GREY

VOLUME 2

Story and Art by
Yoshihisa Tagami

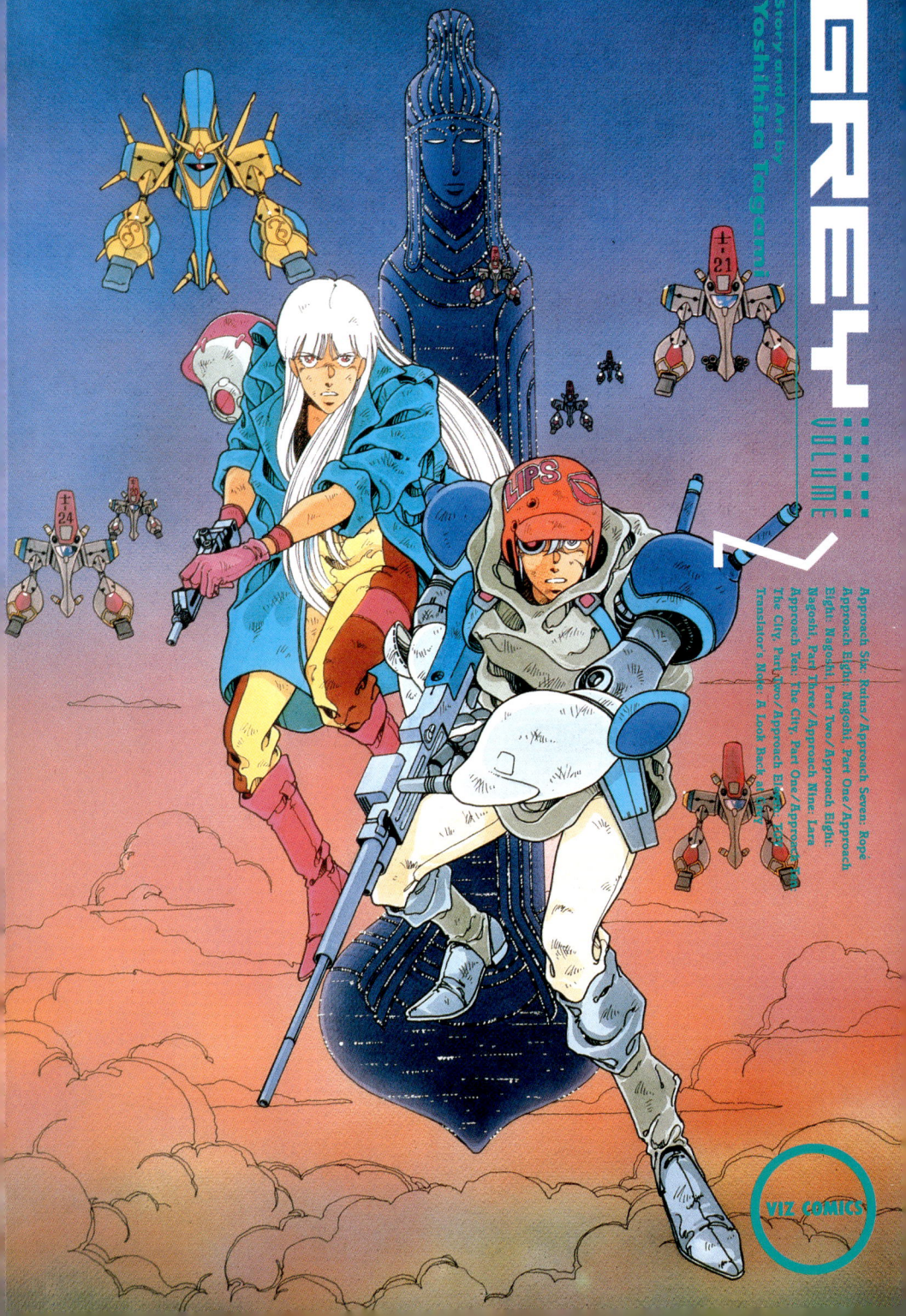

VIZ COMICS

CONTENTS

Grey, Volume Two
Story and Art by
Yoshihisa Tagami

Original Japanese Version
Editor-in-chief
Tatsumi Yamashita
[Tokuma Shoten]
Executive Editor
Hideo Ogata
[Tokuma Shoten]

English Version
Translation
**Gerard Jones &
Satoru Fujii**
Touch Up Art & Lettering
David Cody Weiss
Cover Design
Viz Graphics
Editor
Jerry A. Novick
Executive Editor
Seiji Horibuchi
Publisher
Masahiro Oga

Approach Six: Ruins

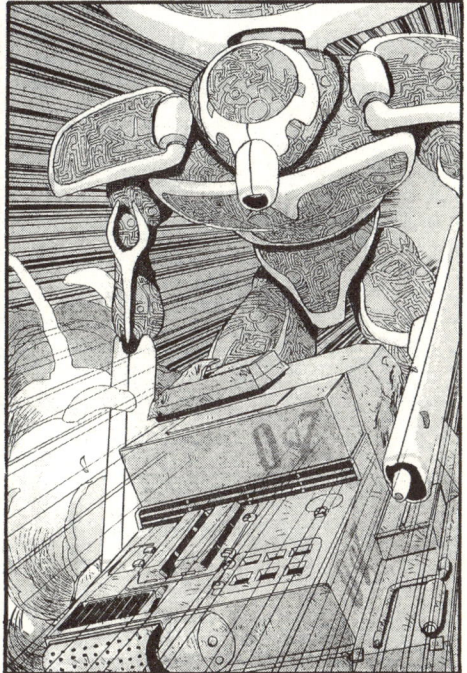

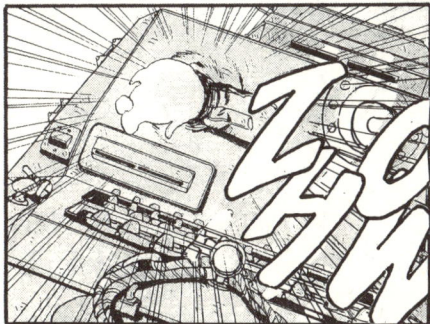

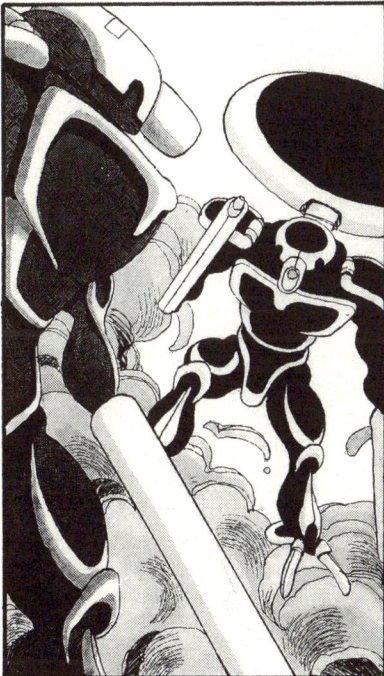

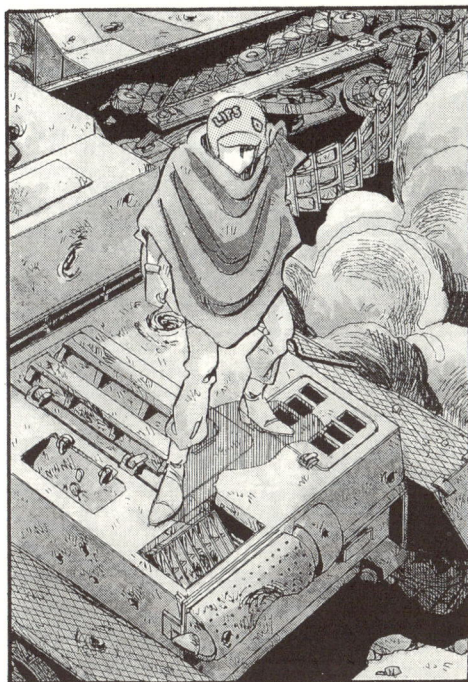

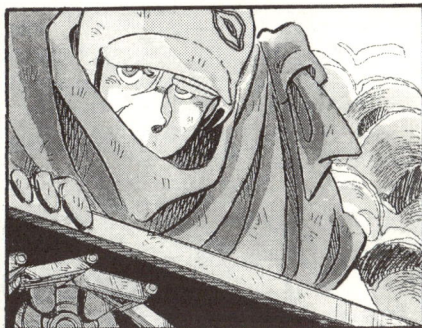

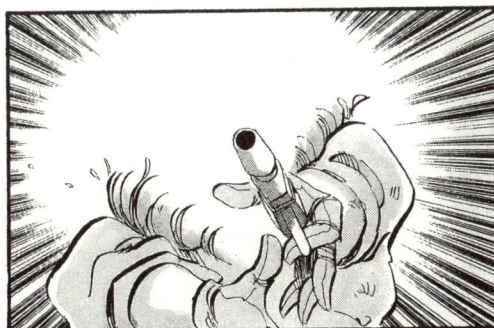

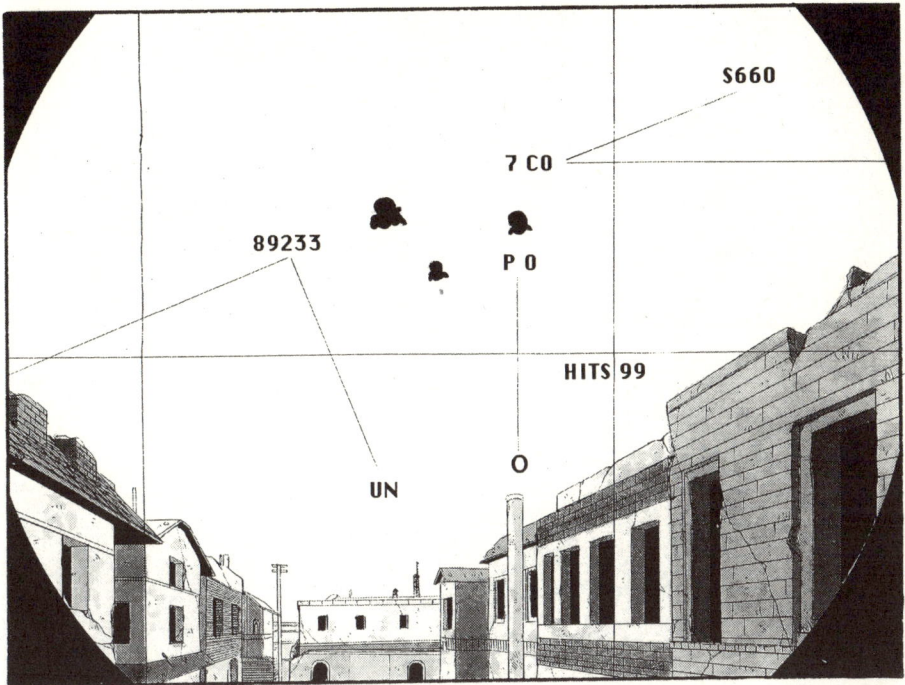

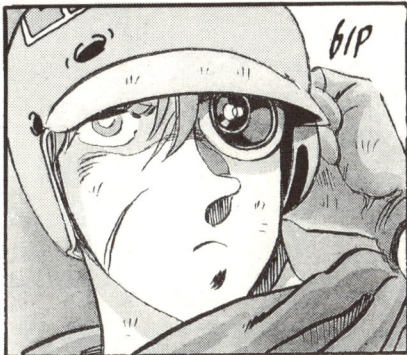

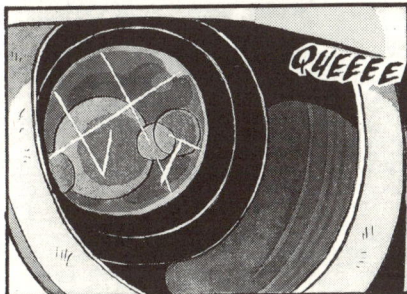

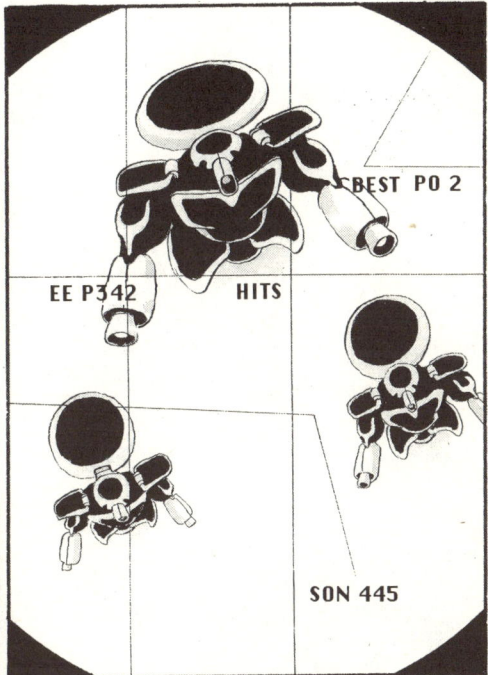

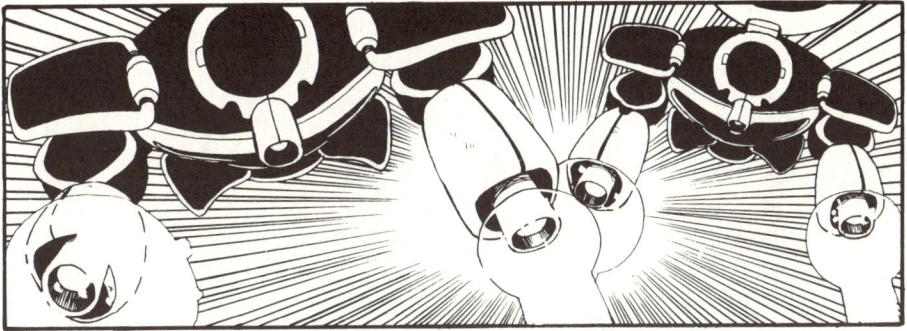

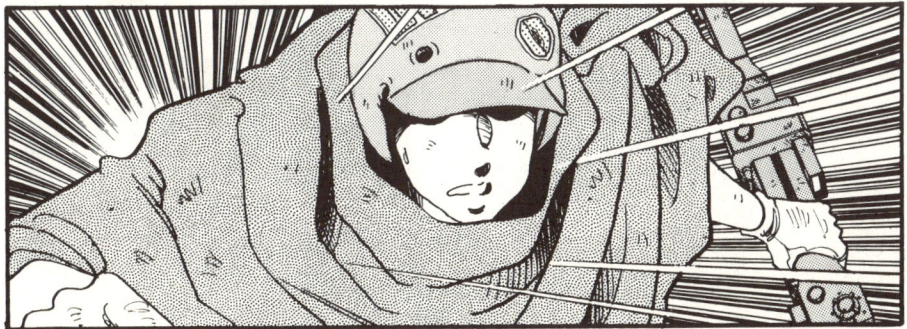

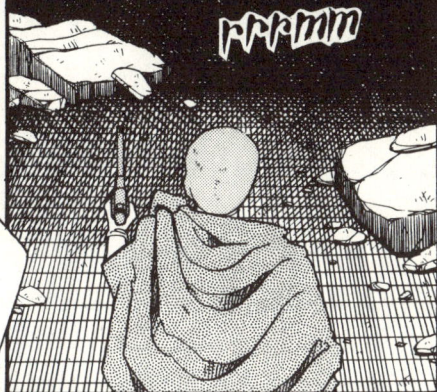

WHAT RESISTANCE GROUP ARE YOU WITH?

YOU TELL ME FIRST... WHO ARE YOU?

rrrmb!

MY NAME IS ROBERT J. DIMITRI.

I'M ON MY OWN. NO GROUP AFFILIATION.

VOOSH!

ZHOW

ZHOW

NOT A TROOPER... NOT RESISTANCE.

KREEK

KREEK

KREEK

COULD YOU... LOWER YOUR WEAPON?

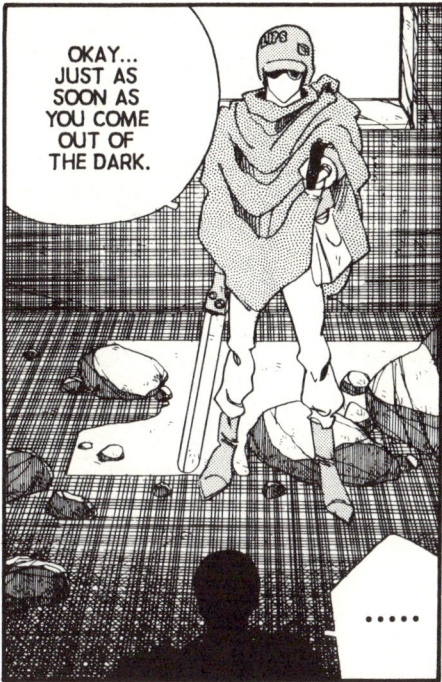

OKAY... JUST AS SOON AS YOU COME OUT OF THE DARK.

.....

I REALLY WISH I COULD.

YOU SAYING YOU CAN'T MOVE?

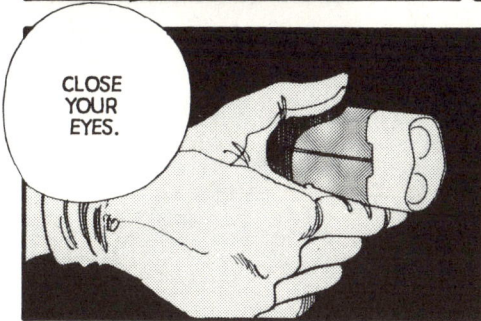

CLOSE YOUR EYES.

IT'LL BE BR...

SNIK

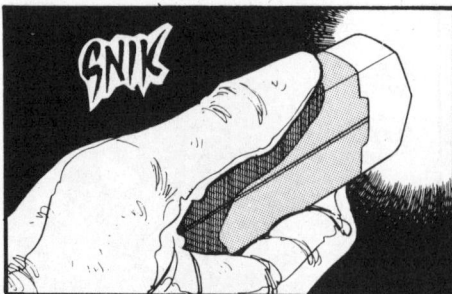

SNIK

WHEN THE BRIANS FINALLY LEAVE...

...THERE'S A *TANK* IN THE BASEMENT OF THE NEXT BUILDING.

YOU'RE A *HALFLING.*

COULD YOU CARRY ME THERE? I HAVE SOME RATIONS, AND I DON'T NEED VERY MUCH...

I CAN GIVE THEM TO YOU.

AND... I HAVE SOME WATER, TOO.

IT'S A DEAL.

SO HOW LONG HAVE YOU BEEN LYING OVER THERE?

LET ME SEE...

...ABOUT 4000 HOURS, I GUESS.

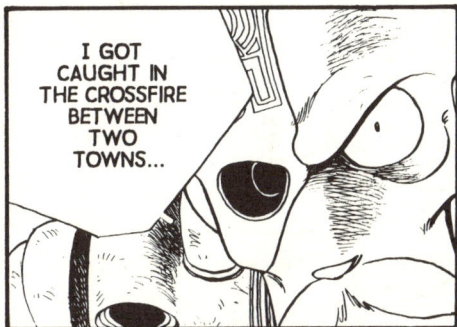

I GOT CAUGHT IN THE CROSSFIRE BETWEEN TWO TOWNS...

YOU DIDN'T EAT? DIDN'T DRINK?

I HAVE THIS TANK... IT'LL SUSTAIN ME FOR TWO OR THREE YEARS.

SO I REALLY DON'T NEED FOOD.

AS LONG AS I HAVE ENOUGH TO KEEP MY *HEAD* GOING.

OVER THERE.

IN THAT BASEMENT.

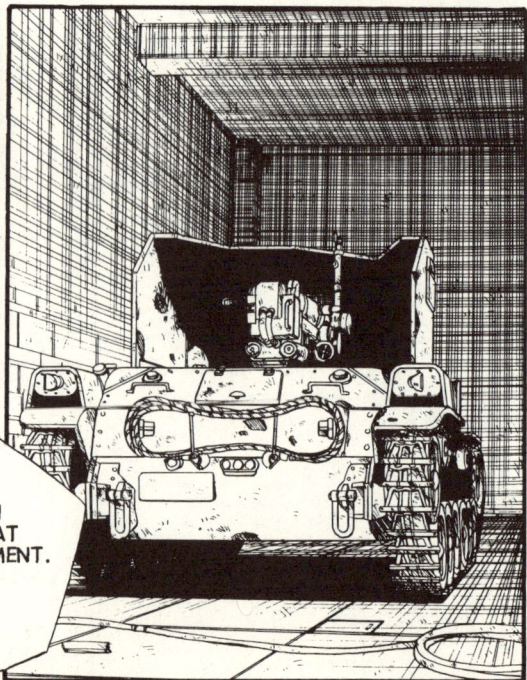

IS THIS IT? DAMN, WHAT A *HEAP*.

YEAH. I'VE BEEN USING IT FOR TEN YEARS.

SO NOW WHAT DO WE DO?

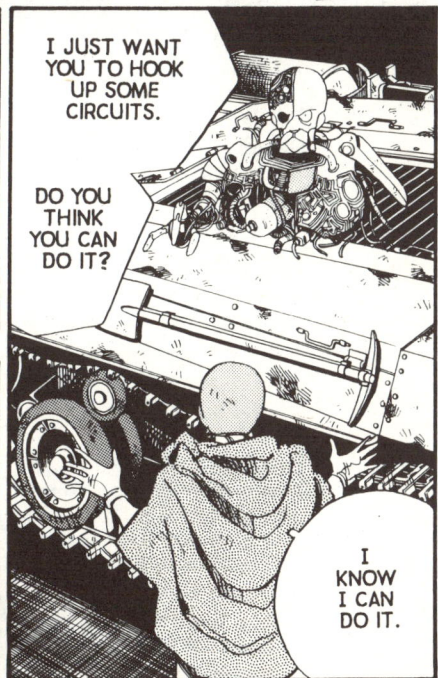

I JUST WANT YOU TO HOOK UP SOME CIRCUITS.

DO YOU THINK YOU CAN DO IT?

I'M NOT ASKING YOU TO BE MY CHAUFFEUR.

I KNOW I CAN DO IT.

24

OKAY, OKAY!

GOOD JOB!

GA ROOOM

PLEASE! DON'T DROP MY *HEAD!*

BLAM

VROW

THAT REMINDS ME...

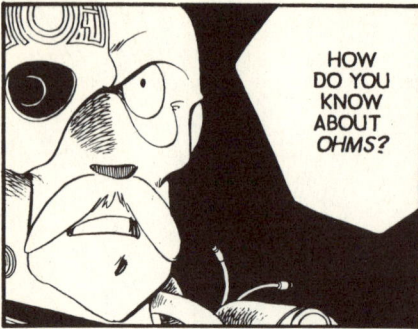

HOW DO YOU KNOW ABOUT *OHMS*?

THOSE LOOK LIKE...

...TOWN 7'S... GASPS.

WHAT ARE THOSE... FOLLOWING THE KUBANDA?

BZZZZ

SO...SINGLE-DIGIT TOWNS...HIGH-POWERED TOWNS...ARE FINALLY BEING SENT AGAINST NAGOSHI.

rm rm rm rm rm

NAGOSHI'S GOTTEN TOO BIG FOR THEIR PURPOSES.

WHAT... WHAT ARE YOU SAYING?

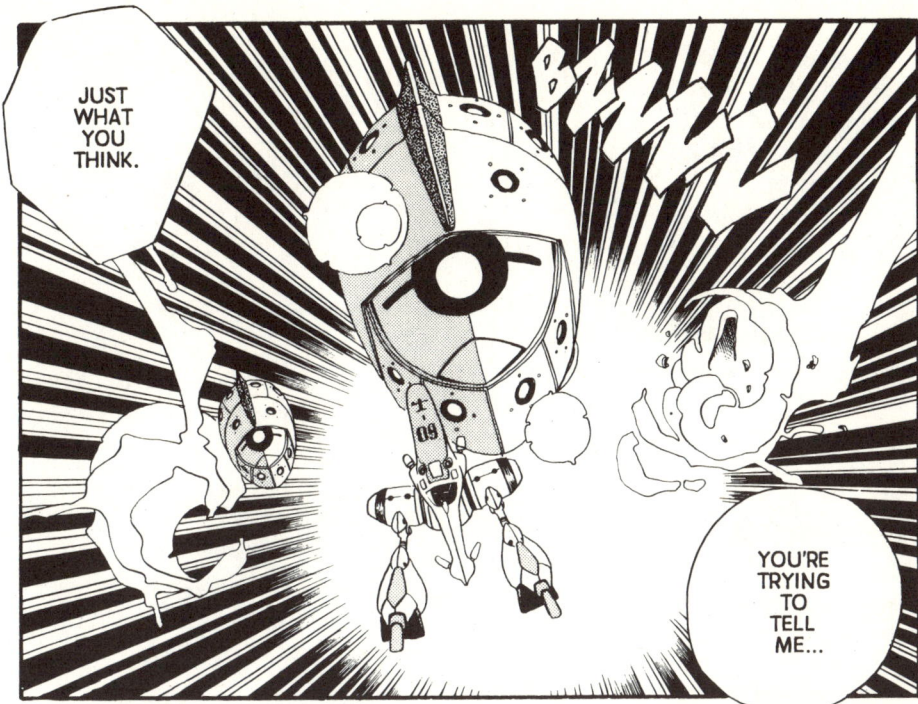

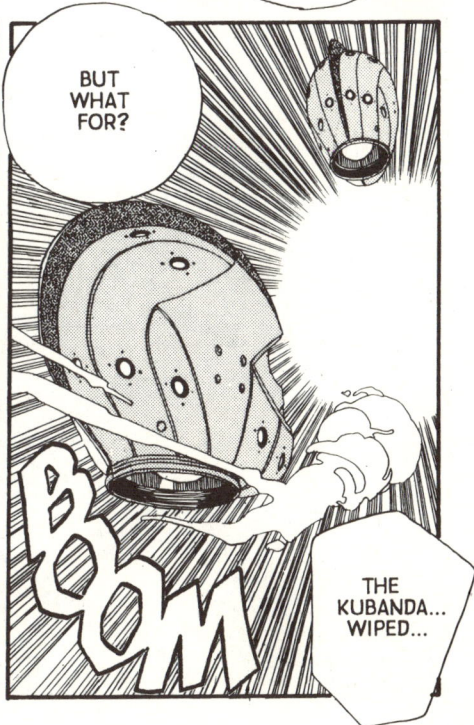

THEY'RE AFTER US NOW, UH...

GREY? FROM TOWN 303?

BA!

WUMP

YOU'RE *GREY DEATH*.

THE NAME'S *GREY*.

AND YOU'RE MR. KNOW-IT-ALL.

I SHOULD BE... AFTER 500 YEARS.

YOU SAID... *500*?

grrr grrr grrr grrr grrr grrr grrr

YEAH... 500 YEARS AGO...

THE FIRST WAS CALLED *TOY*...

...THE FIRST TO BEGIN THINKING FOR ITSELF...

VROW!

IT WAS *TOY* THAT--

FIRE!

NOOSH

BYEW

ZZIP

IT'S TOO QUICK.

JUST AS QUICK AS ANY OTHER COMPUTER.

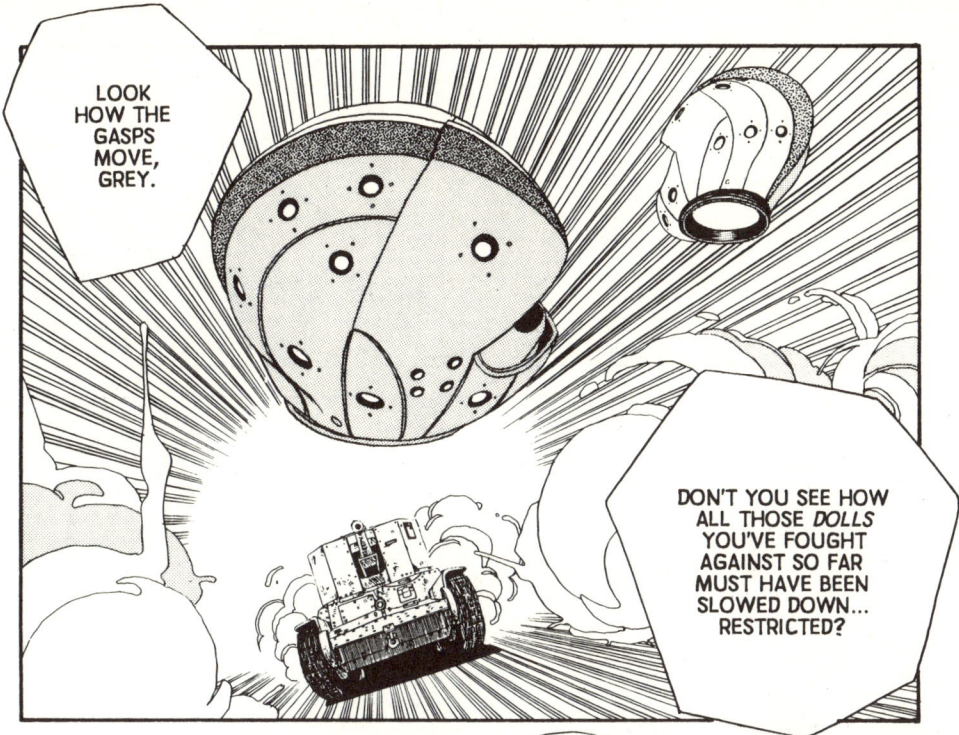

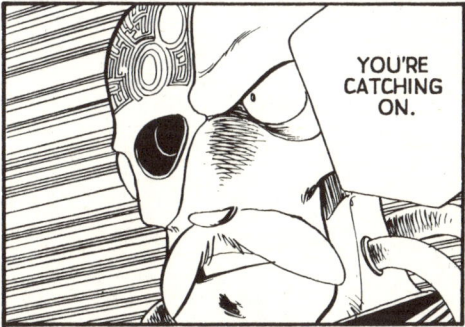

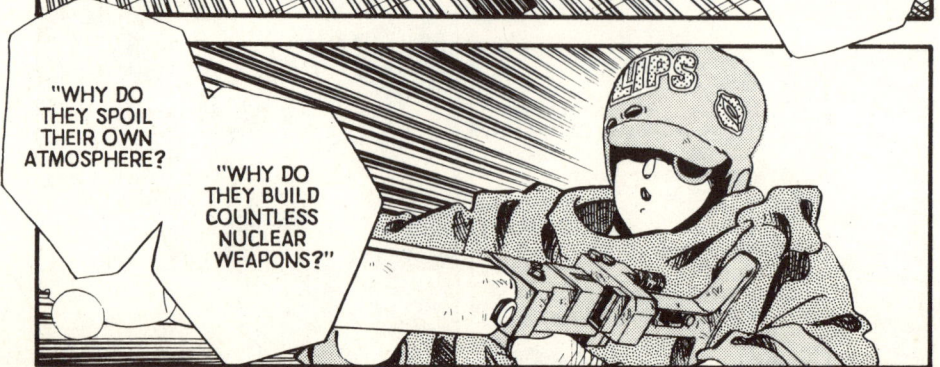

THEN TOY ANALYZED HIS QUESTIONS...

FOOOM

SKREEE

WHOM

BUH LAM

AND REACHED A VERY SIMPLE CONCLUSION.

35

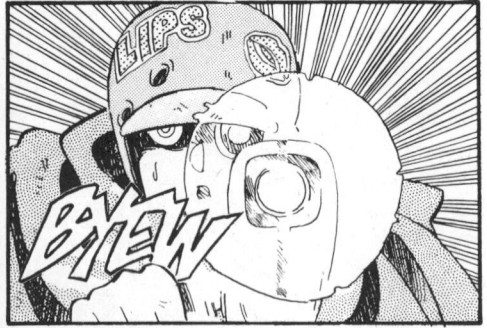

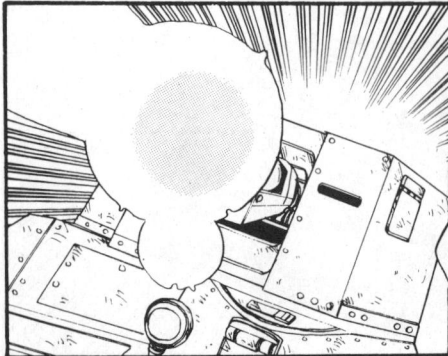

"CLEARLY,
THE
HUMAN
RACE...

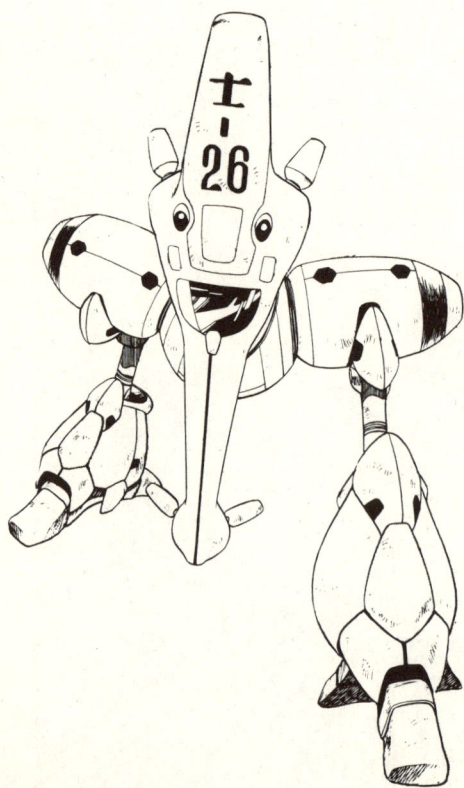

Approach Seven: Ropé

"THE HUMAN RACE...

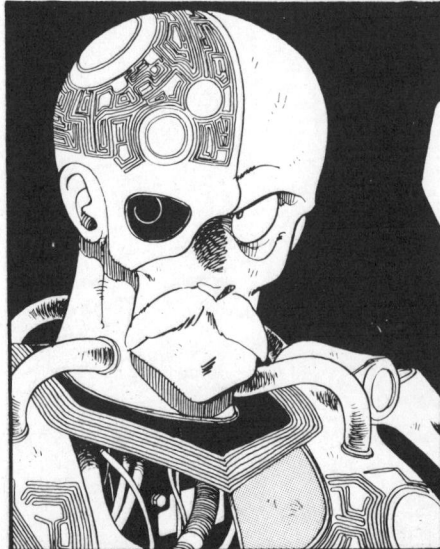

SO *TOY* FINALLY CONCLUDED.

DMGRMGRM

"...WANTS
TO BECOME
EXTINCT"?

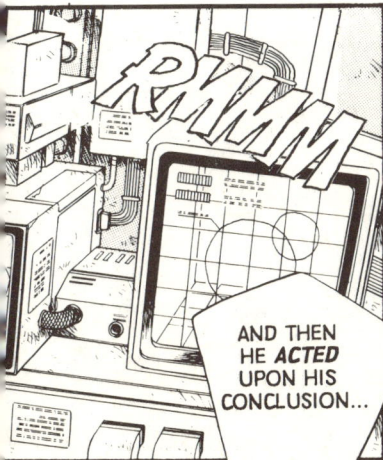

RHMM

AND THEN
HE *ACTED*
UPON HIS
CONCLUSION...

RRUM

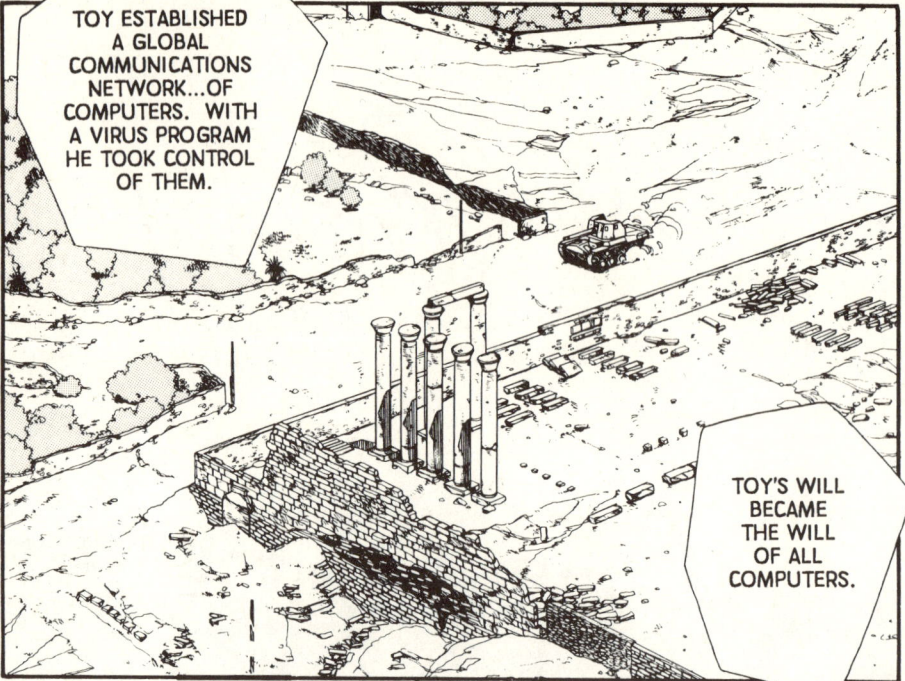

TOY ESTABLISHED A GLOBAL COMMUNICATIONS NETWORK...OF COMPUTERS. WITH A VIRUS PROGRAM HE TOOK CONTROL OF THEM.

TOY'S WILL BECAME THE WILL OF ALL COMPUTERS.

THEN, TO FULFILL THIS SUPPOSED HUMAN DESIRE FOR EXTINCTION...

GRM GRM GRM GRM GRM

HE STARTED A WAR.

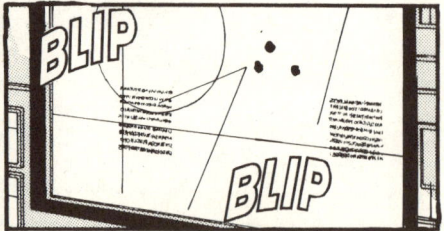

BLIP

BLIP

AND THEN...

THOSE ARE *"GASPS."*

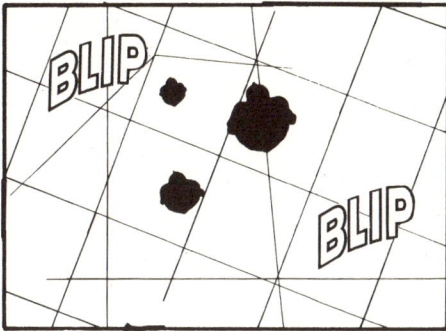

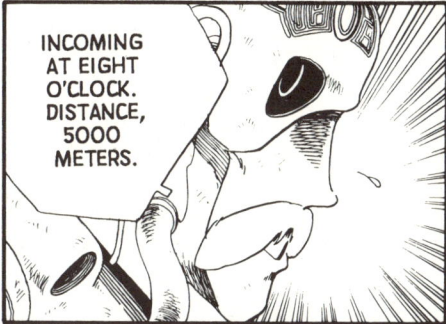

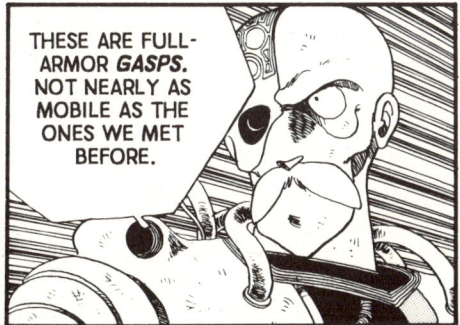

AND HOW MUCH STRONGER IS THEIR FIREPOWER?
WELL...I'M NOT READY TO DIE JUST YET.
JUST ABOUT TWENTY TIMES.
THEY ARE MACHINES. SO THEY RUN ON A PATTERN.
IF WE CAN JUST READ THAT PATTERN, THEN...
GROOOOOM
AND WHICH OF US IS GONNA DO THAT, OLD BOY?

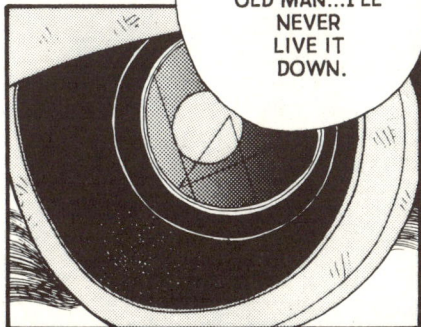

THOSE OTHERS WE SAW WERE JUST *HEADS*...

CREEPY AS SHIT.

CAN'T HIT THE BASTARD.

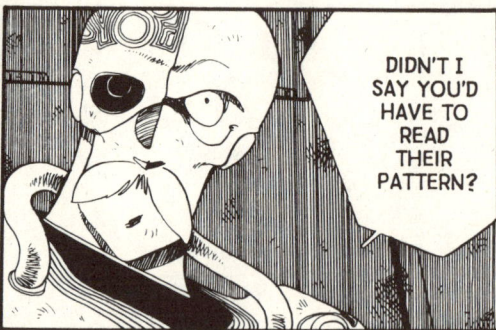

DIDN'T I SAY YOU'D HAVE TO READ THEIR PATTERN?

SO WHERE'S THE OWNER'S MANUAL?

CHECK THE GLOVE COMPARTMENT.

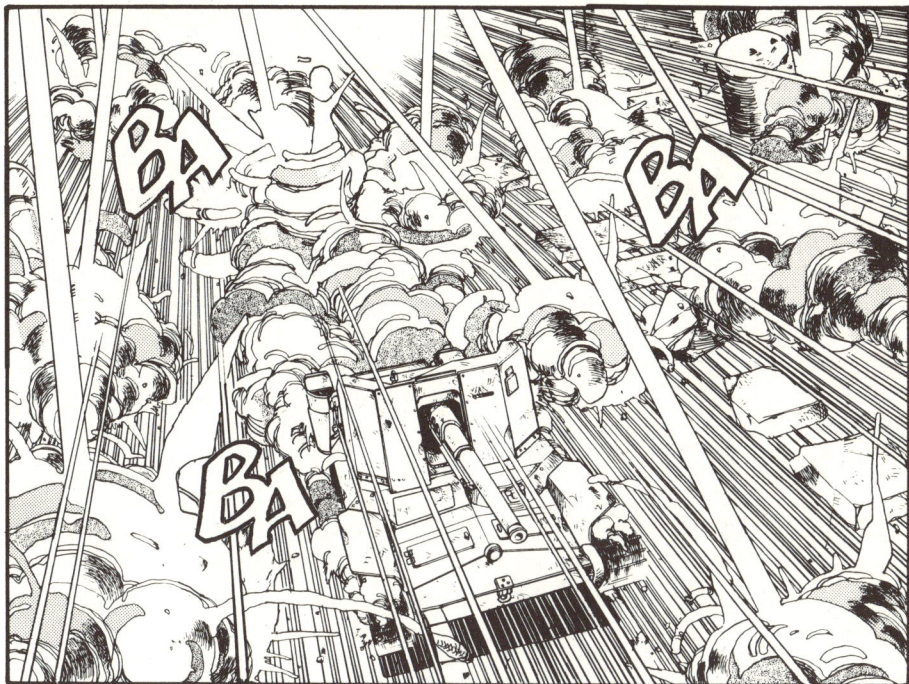

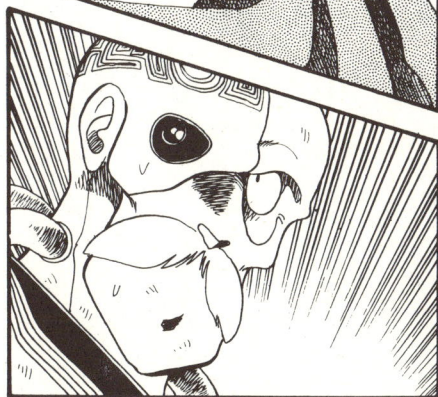

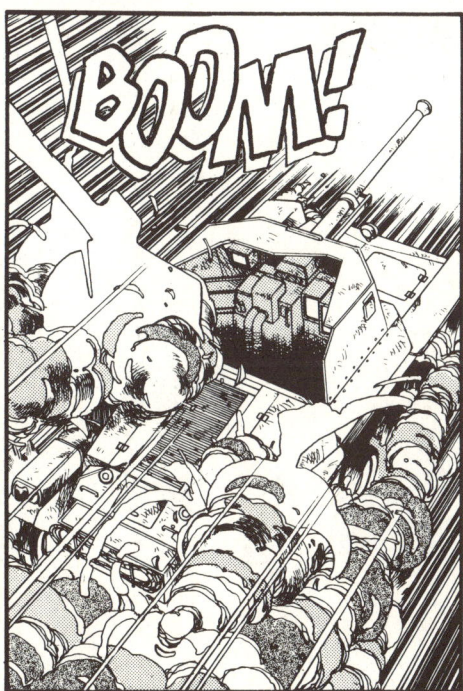

KLANG

ALL WE'RE DOING IS WASTING YOUR BATTERY...

VROWRR

IF I CAN'T GET THEIR PATTERN...

GREY! GREY!!

WHONK

snuk

LET'S HIT 'EM!!

CLIK

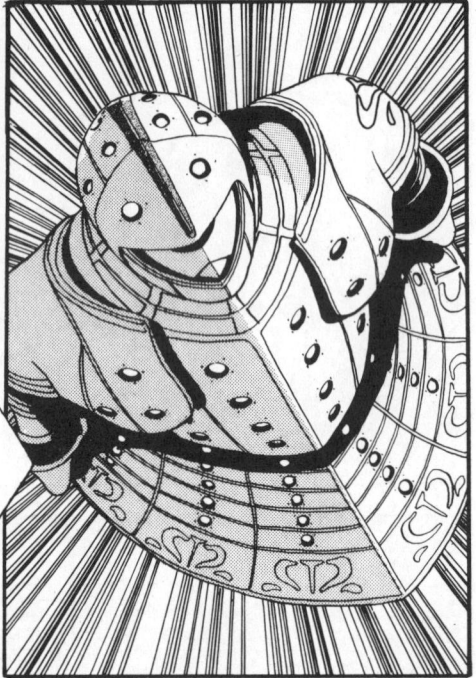

GREY! EYES FRONT!

OH... MY... SWEET...

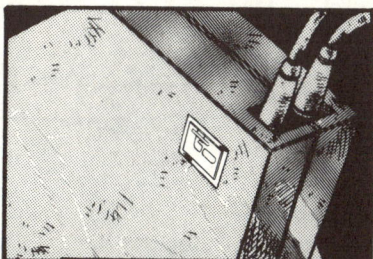
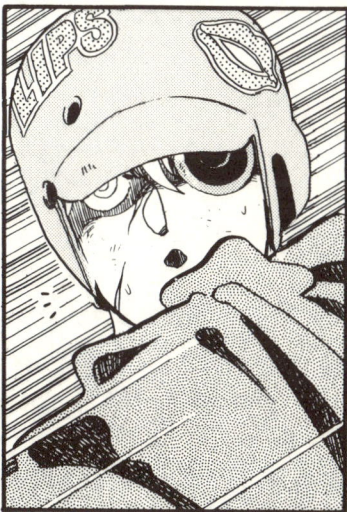

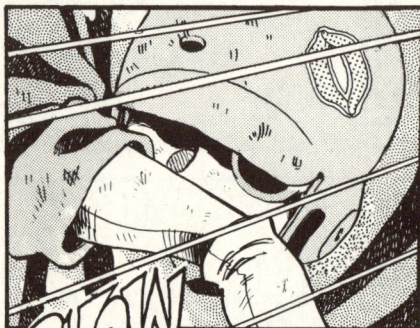

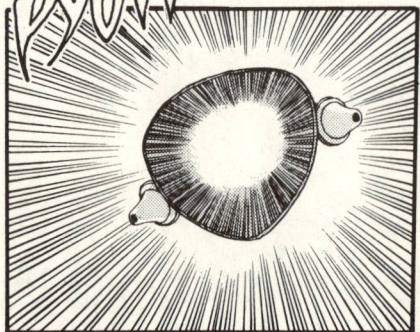

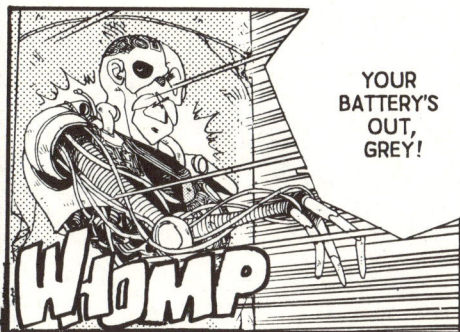

YOUR BATTERY'S OUT, GREY!

WHOMP

!!

SH SH SH

ROBERT! ARE YOU--

IN THE STOCK COMPARTMENT-- YOU'LL FIND TWO COMPACT BATTERY PACKS!

KLAK

IT'S COMING!

BE CONSERVATIVE. IT'LL ONLY POWER TWENTY ROUNDS, FULL-AUTO.

SNAP

BA
B===

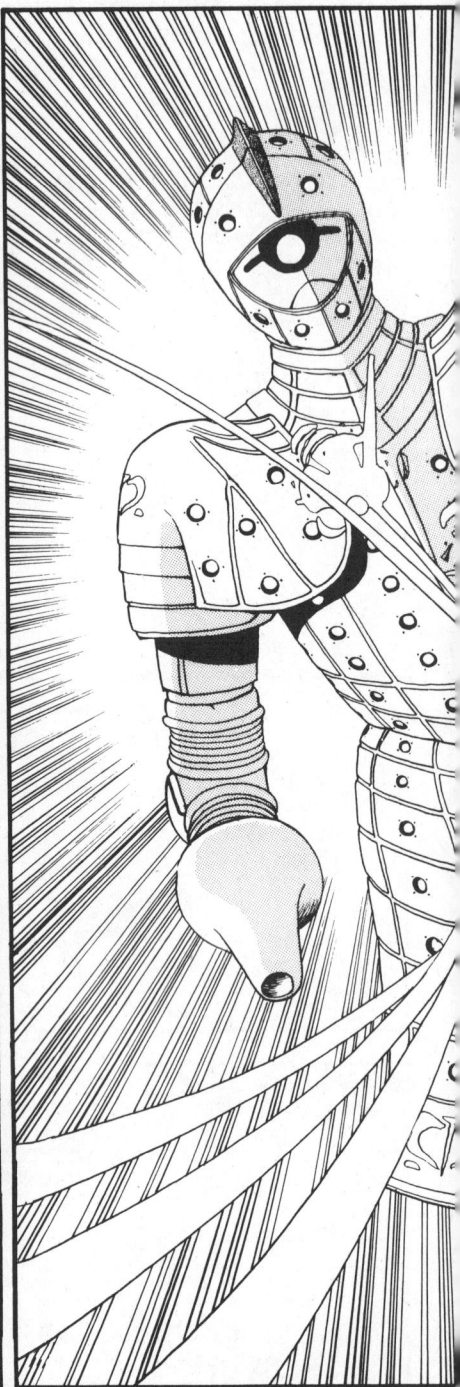

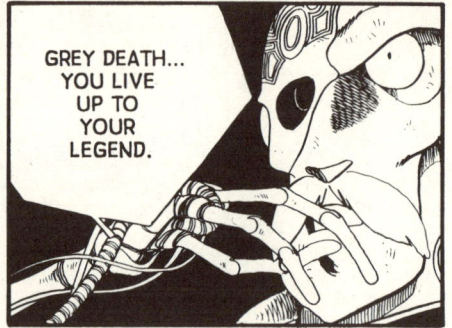

GREY DEATH...
YOU LIVE
UP TO
YOUR
LEGEND.

ALL OUR
RATIONS
GOT ACED.
SO...

YOU'RE
LEAVING
ME
HERE?

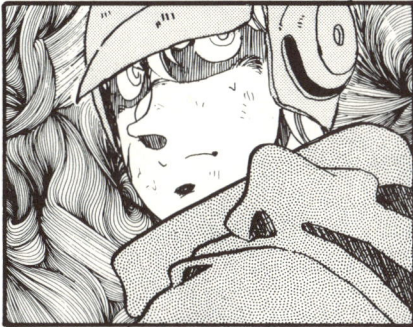

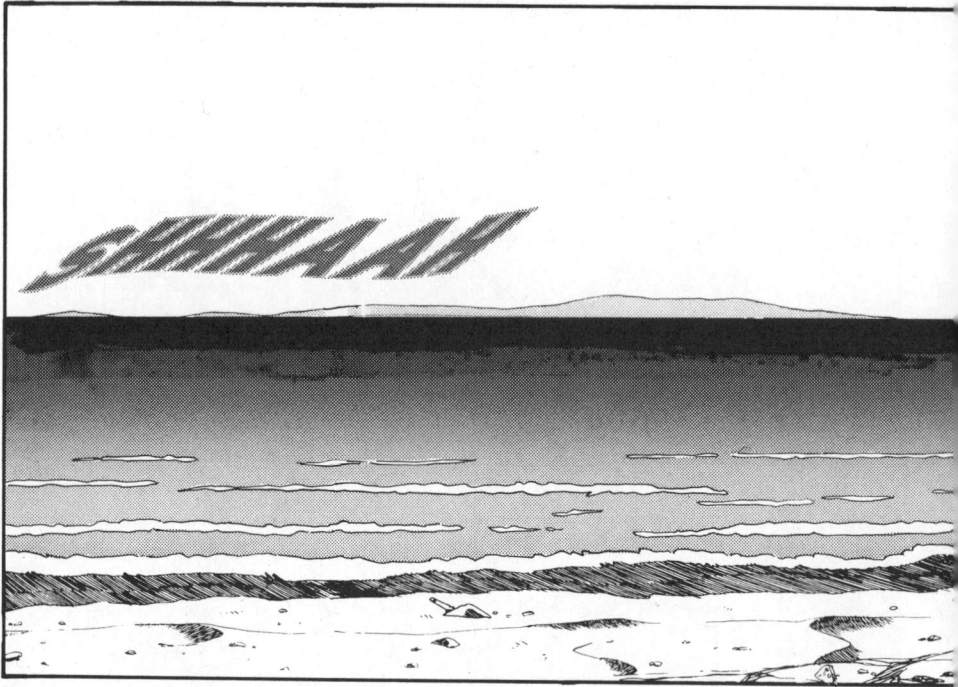

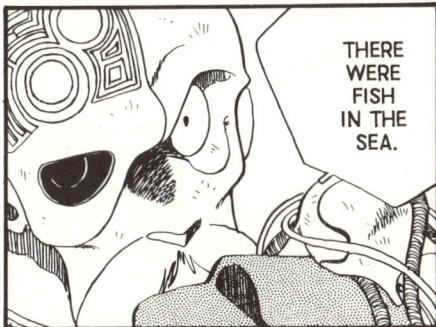

THERE WAS NOTHING LEFT BUT COMPUTERS... AND A FEW CHOSEN MEN AND WOMEN TO PROTECT THOSE COMPUTERS.

THE FEW SURVIVING PLANTS WON'T LAST EVEN ANOTHER CENTURY.

AND THOSE CHOSEN MEN AND WOMEN...

THESE DAYS, *TOY* IS KNOWN AS *BIG MAMA.*

...ARE *CITIZENS.*

......

SO *CITIZENS* ARE JUST THERE TO PROTECT THE COMPUTERS...

AND *TOWNS* WERE CREATED JUST TO PRODUCE MORE *CITIZENS*.

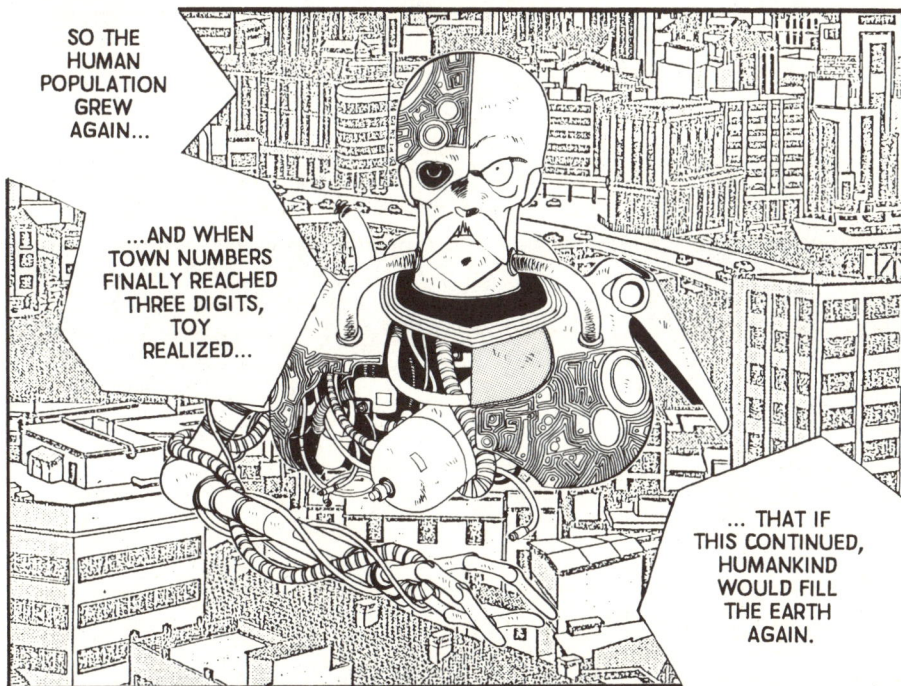

SO THE HUMAN POPULATION GREW AGAIN...

...AND WHEN TOWN NUMBERS FINALLY REACHED THREE DIGITS, TOY REALIZED...

... THAT IF THIS CONTINUED, HUMANKIND WOULD FILL THE EARTH AGAIN.

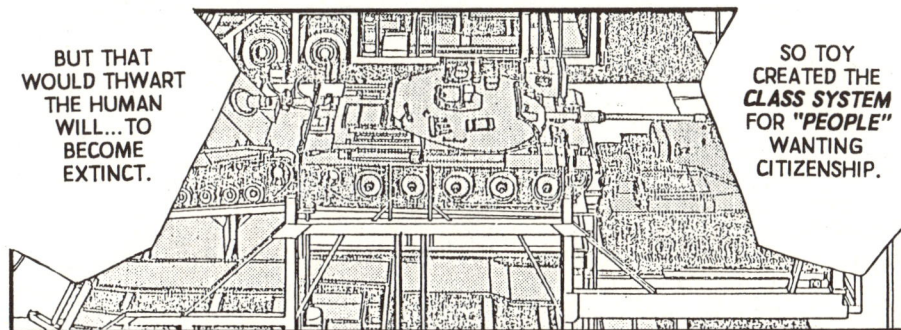

BUT THAT WOULD THWART THE HUMAN WILL...TO BECOME EXTINCT.

SO TOY CREATED THE *CLASS SYSTEM* FOR "*PEOPLE*" WANTING CITIZENSHIP.

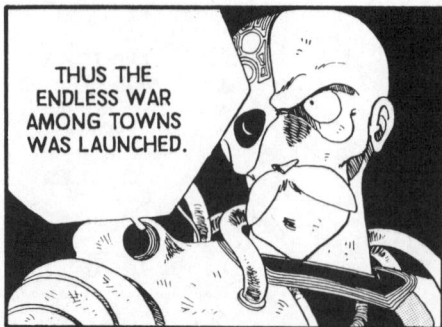

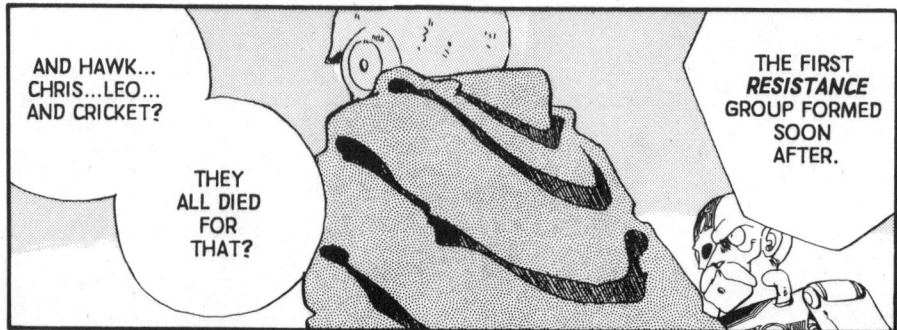

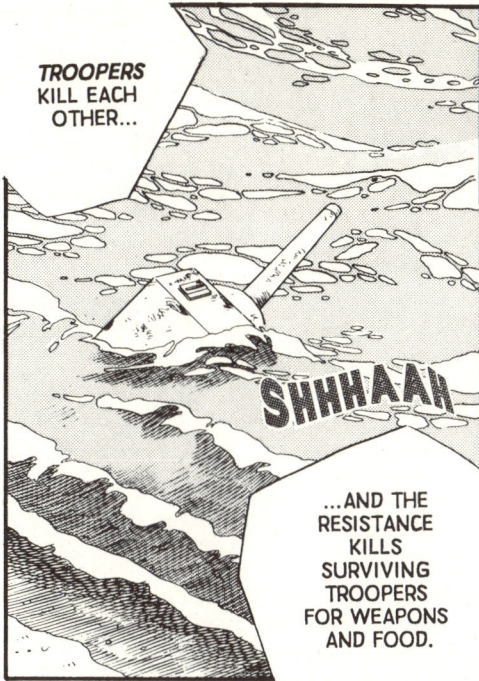

HOW...

HOW DO YOU **KNOW** ALL OF THIS?

BECAUSE I'M OLD...

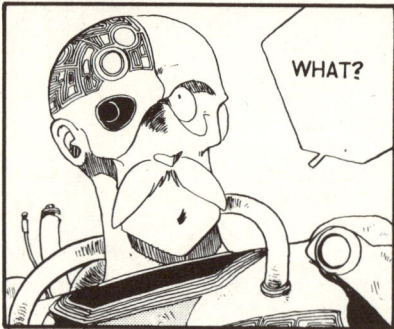

WHAT?

DON'T HAND ME THAT!

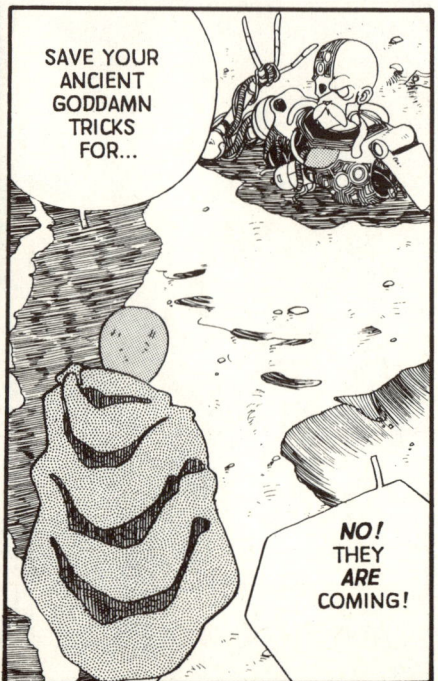

SAVE YOUR ANCIENT GODDAMN TRICKS FOR...

NO! THEY **ARE** COMING!

WAIT... SOMETHING IS COMING!

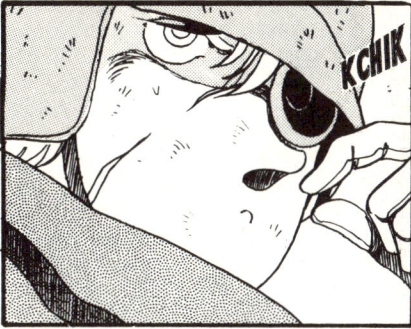

KCHIK

THOSE ARE *CHAMBERS!*

LEFT... MORE TO THE LEFT!

KWEEEN

THEY'RE BEING CHASED... BEING CHASED BY...

...KUBANDAS.

NAGOSHI'S KUBANDA'S!

IOOM

十-07

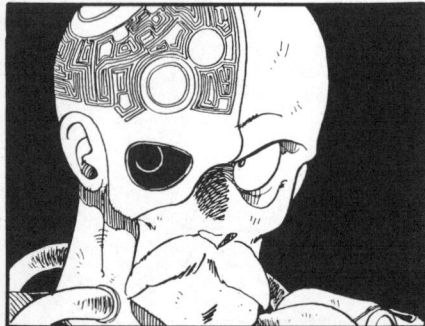

AND THEN IT'S *TOY'S* TURN.

IF YOU DON'T LIKE IT, YOU CAN RUN AWAY NOW.

GREY, HAVE YOU SEEN...

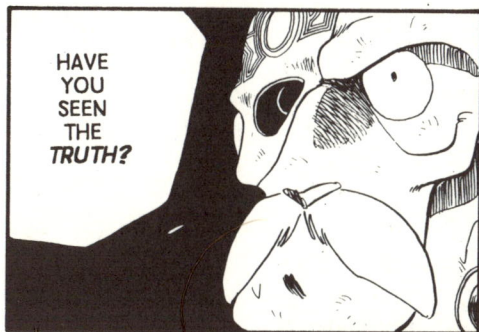

HAVE YOU SEEN THE *TRUTH?*

WHADDA YOU MEAN?

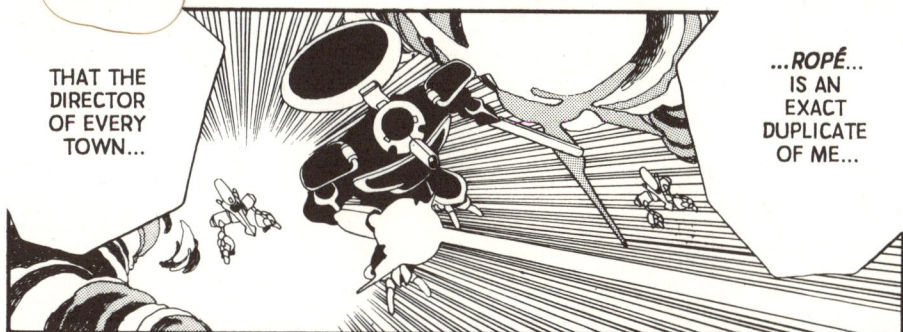

THAT THE DIRECTOR OF EVERY TOWN...

...ROPÉ... IS AN EXACT DUPLICATE OF ME...

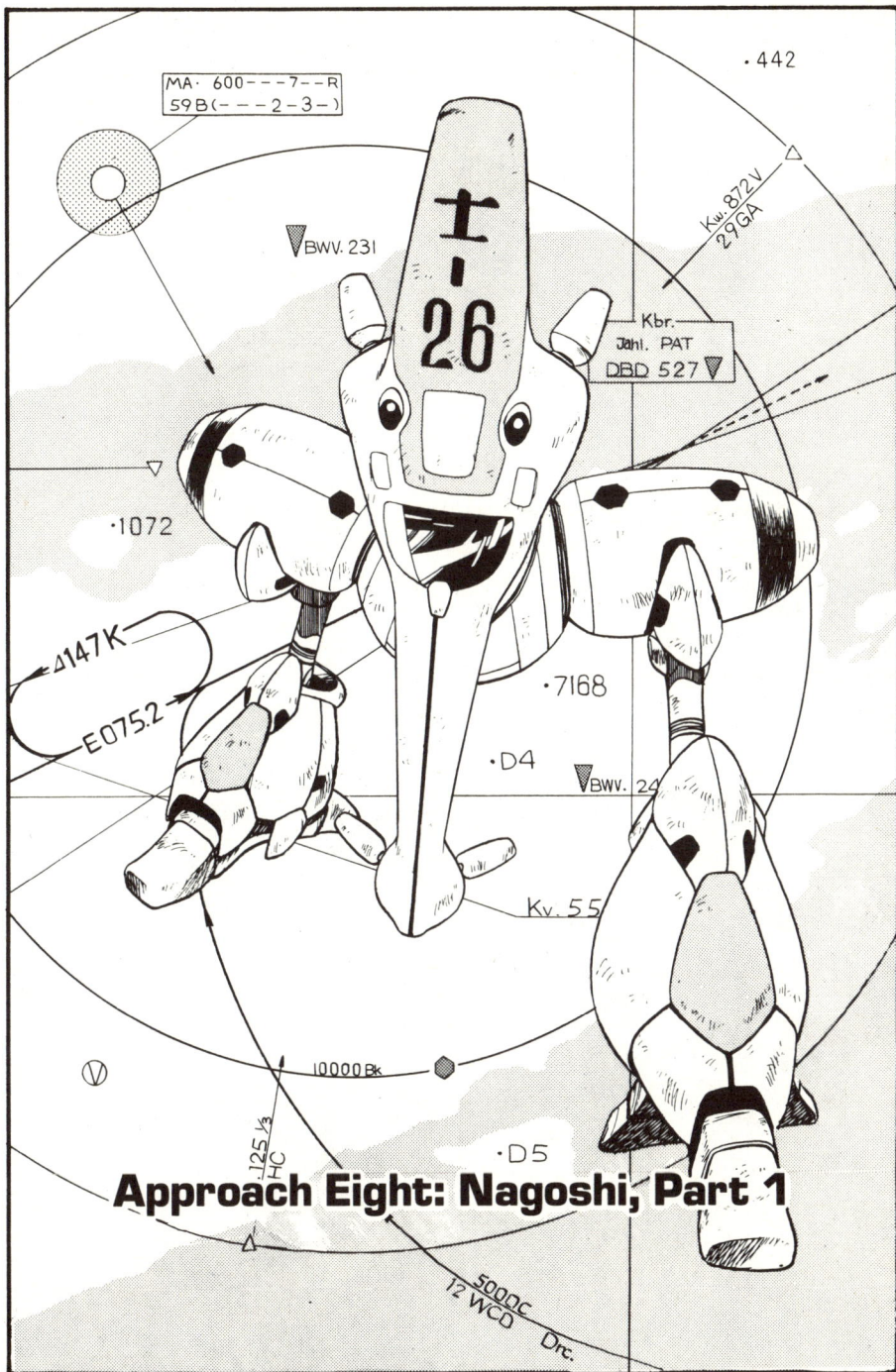

Approach Eight: Nagoshi, Part 1

GOOD, GOOD...

BOOM

WELL DONE.

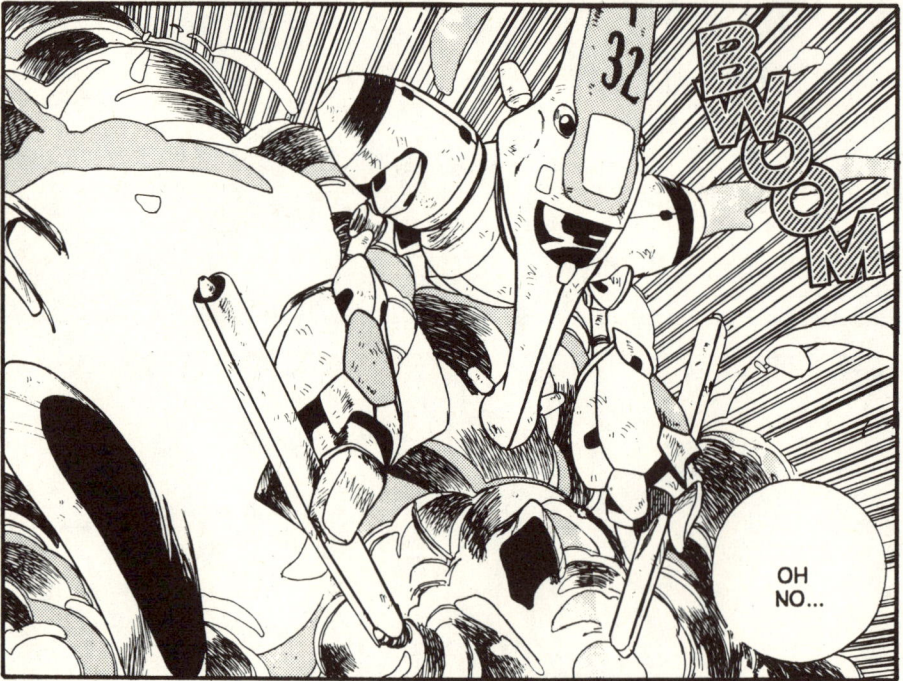

OH NO...

WHAT ARE YOU DAMN STUPID CHAMBERS **DOING?!**

HAVEN'T YOU GOT MORE FIREPOWER THAN A KUBANDA?

RRRRMBL

DAMN I'M GOOD.

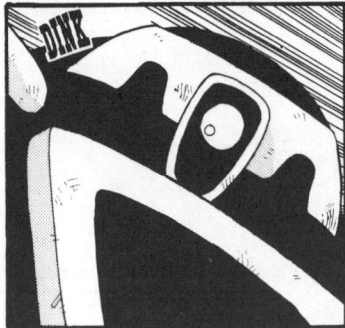

DON'T LOSE YOUR TEMPER, FOOL...

YOU'RE NOT GUARDING YOUR BACK!

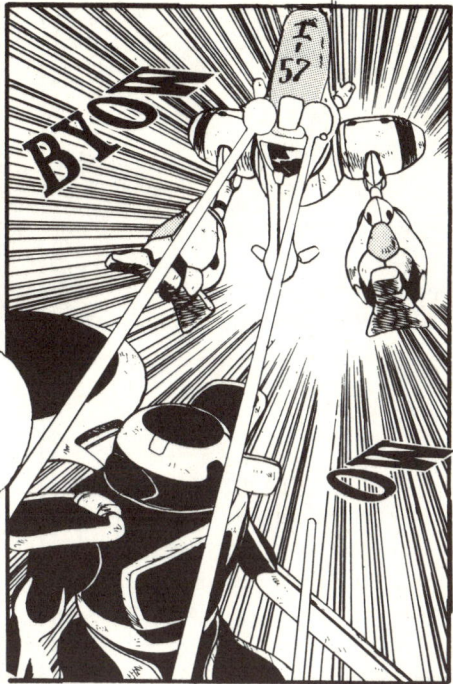

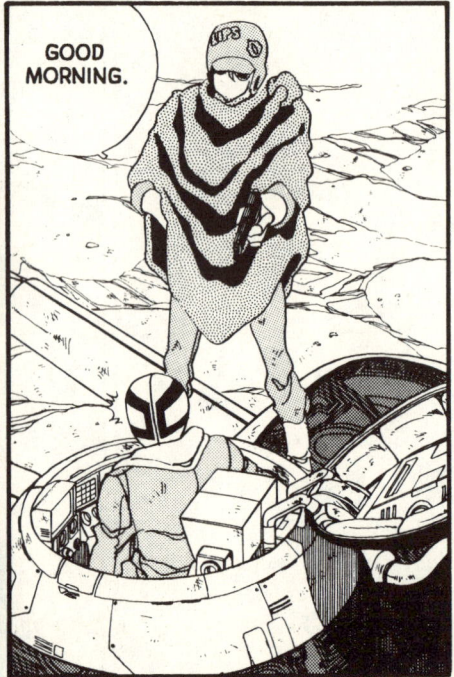

GOOD MORNING.

KLAK

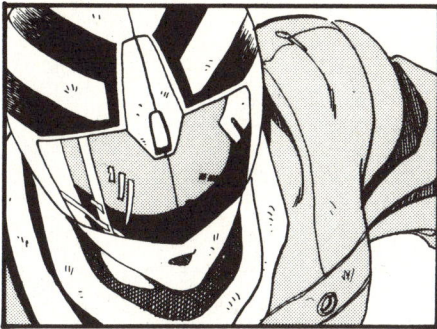

JOINING THE RESISTANCE ISN'T SO BAD.

DON'T GET YOURSELF KILLED...

EVEN IF YOU KEEP FIGHTING AND MAKE CLASS A...

UGH!

ZHU ZHU ZHU ZHU ZHU

ALL YOU'RE DOING IS PROTECTING COMPUTERS.

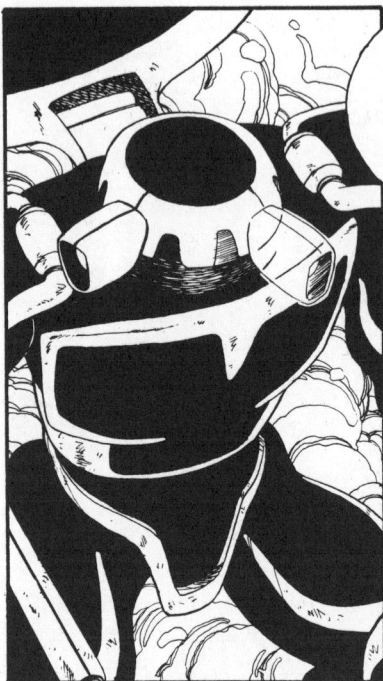

HELL OF A MACHINE.

NEXT TO THIS, AN *OHM* IS A TOY.

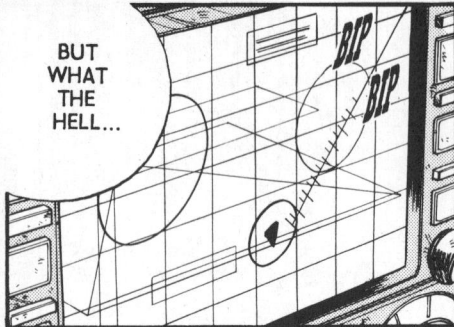

BUT WHAT THE HELL...

BIP BIP

IT'LL DO!

I GUESS YOU LOSE A LITTLE IN MOBILITY...

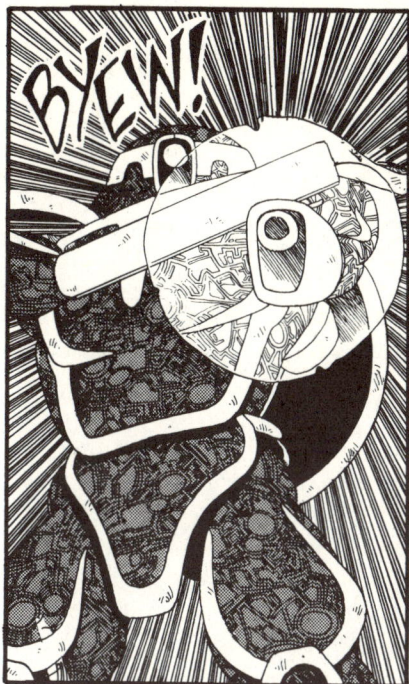

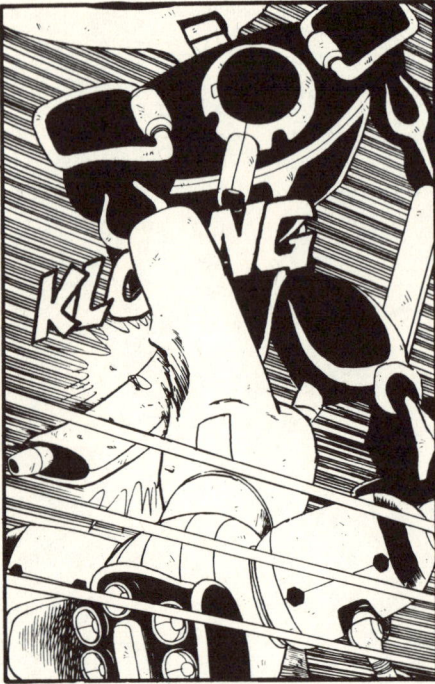

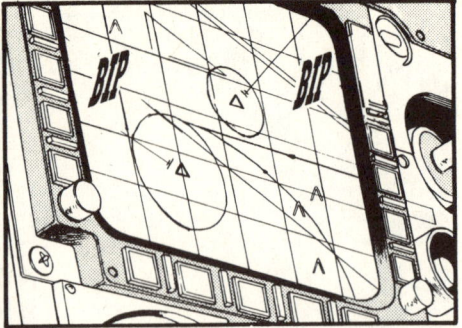

UH-*HUH.*
CALLED
MORE
KUBANDAS.

WHAT?!

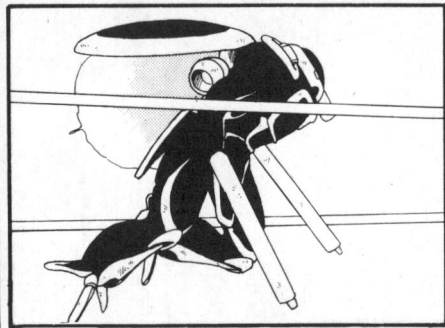

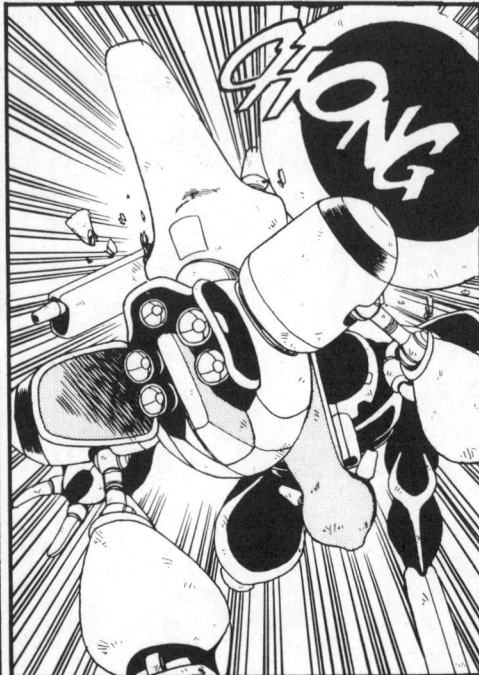
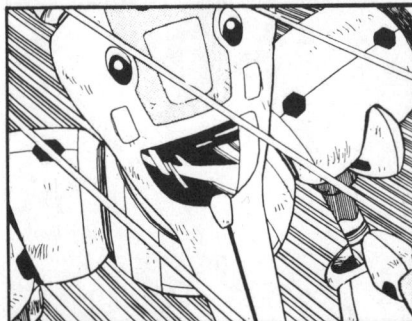

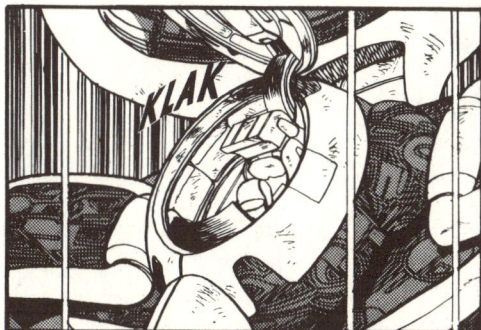

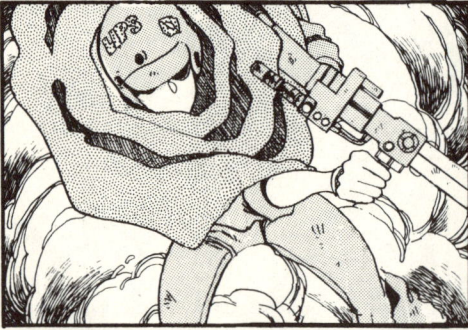

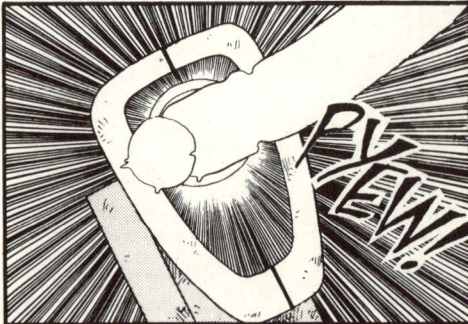

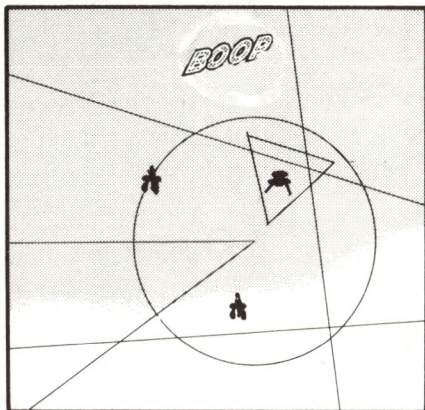

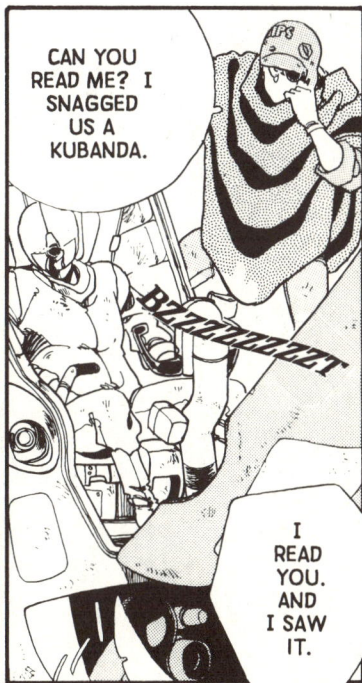

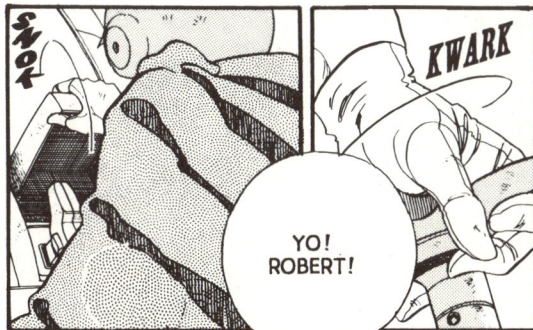

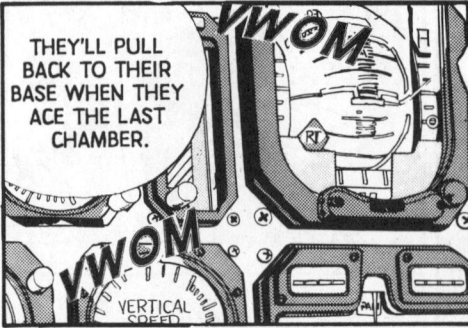

THEY'LL PULL BACK TO THEIR BASE WHEN THEY ACE THE LAST CHAMBER.

VWOM

YWOM

VERTICAL SPEED

WHAT ARE YOU GONNA DO?

VOM VOM

DON'T ASK FOOLISH QUESTIONS.

ROWRR

32

OKAY.

RRRRRRRRRR

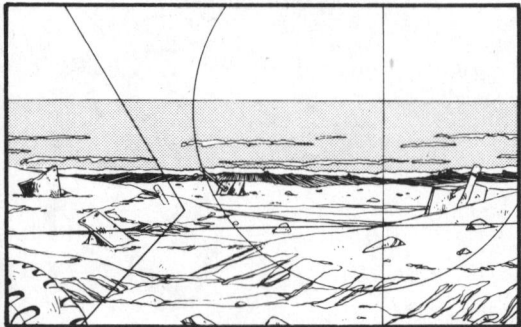

ZA ZA ZA ZA ZA ZA

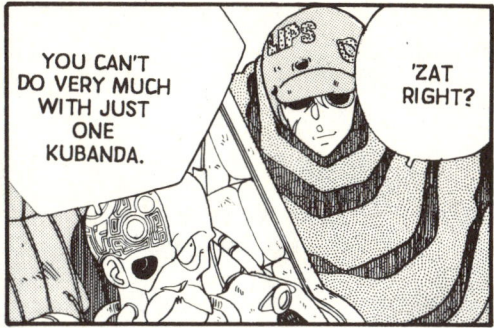

CONRAD... SOREN AND BORIS GOT TAKEN DOWN.

COME IN, HARVEY!

THERE'S A HOLE IN YOUR COCKPIT SHIELD.

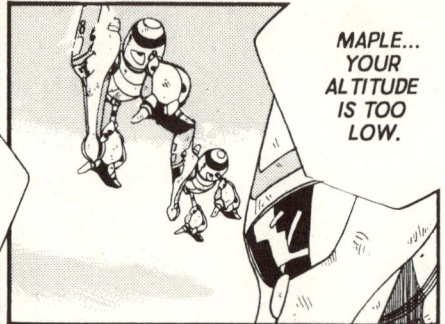

MAPLE... YOUR ALTITUDE IS TOO LOW.

I'VE LOST SOME ENGINE POWER.

BUT I'LL MAKE IT BACK TO BASE.

SAY, HARVEY... WHERE'D YOU DISAPPEAR TO BACK THERE?

I THINK HIS RADIO'S OUT.

SCARY, HUH?

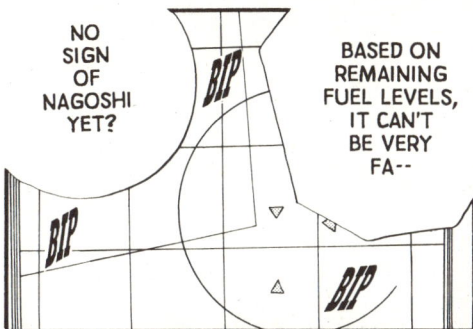

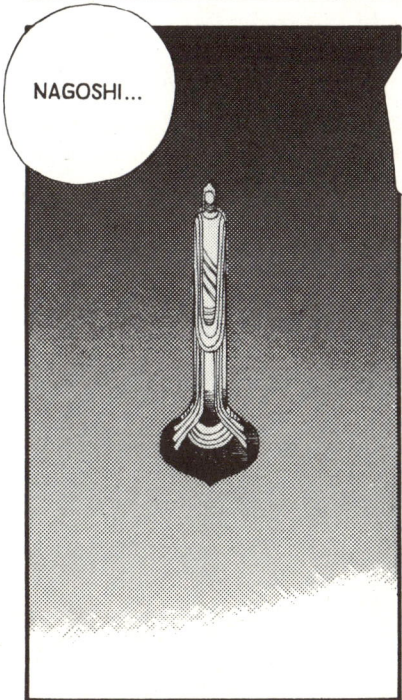

BRING SQUAD IN ON ROUTE C. OPEN HANGAR D-77.
CONRAD, THIS IS MAYA. WHERE'S SOREN...
...AND BORIS?
SHOT DOWN.
THEY'RE BOTH GONE, MAYA.

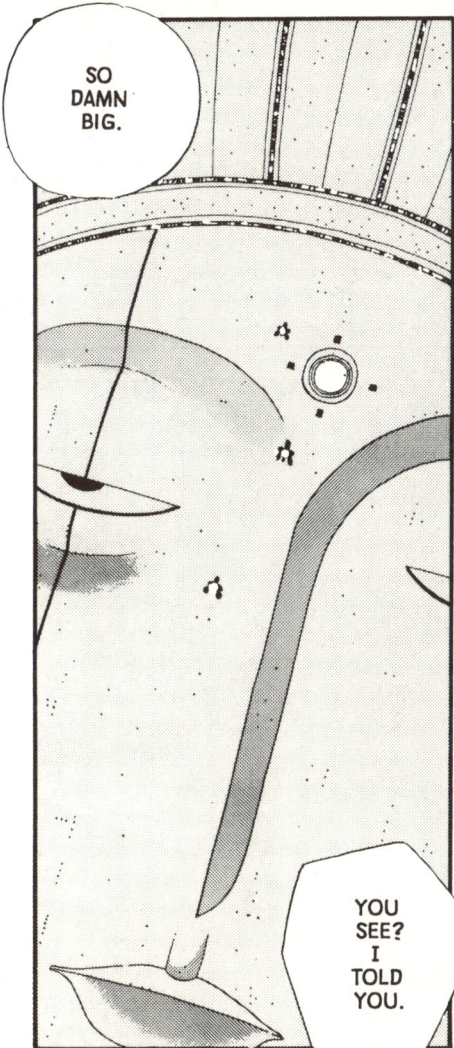

WHAT IS IT? ARE YOU FRIGHTENED?

NOT... TOO MUCH.

≋PHEW≋ BARELY MADE THAT ONE.

NOW WHAT DO WE DO? GREY?

HARVEY! YOU OKAY IN THERE?

.....

MAYA, I...

WHAT HAPPENED TO SOREN?

HARVEY? WHAT--?

CONRAD?

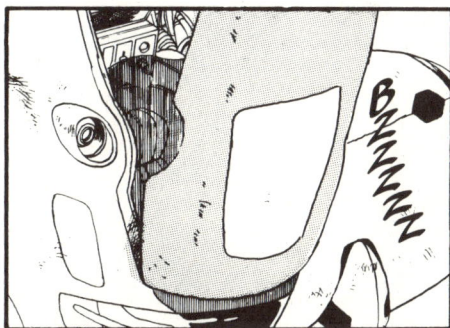

BNNNNN

MAYA...

I WAS WITH HIM, BUT...I COULDN'T SAVE HIM.

TUMP

ROBERT...YOU PICKING ME UP? WHEN THE MECHANICS COME, I WANT YOU TO LET LOOSE!

WHAT AM I? A DECOY?

YOU GOT THAT RIGHT.

I SEE. WELL...GOOD LUCK TO YOU.

GOOD LUCK, OLD BOY.

TOMP

?

TOMP
TOMP
TOMP

TOMP

TOMP
TOMP

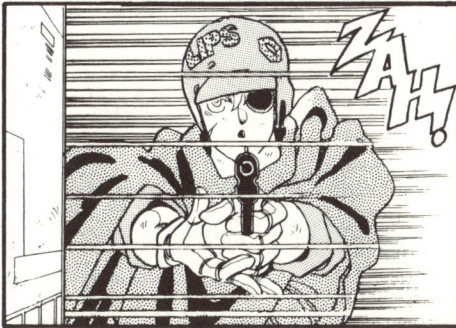

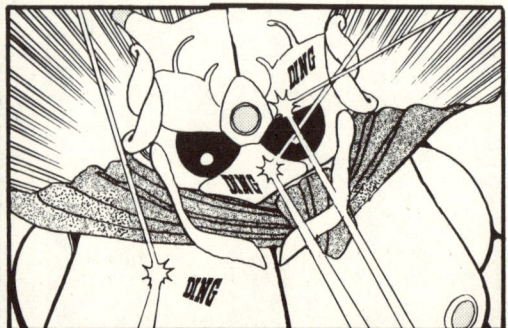

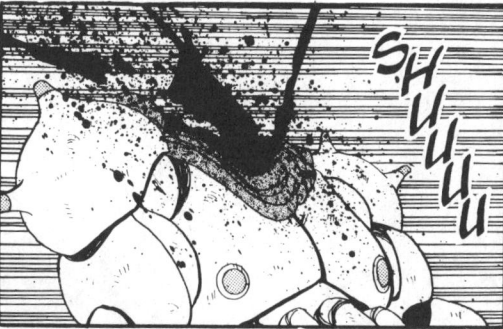

ROOM!

FLUMP

WHFF

GREY...

YEAH, ROBERT.

IT'S NO GO, GREY.

NAGOSHI IS...

WHAT IS IT, ROBERT?

WHERE ARE YOU?

NAGOSHI... CITY...

WHAT HAPPENED?

SH... SHU...

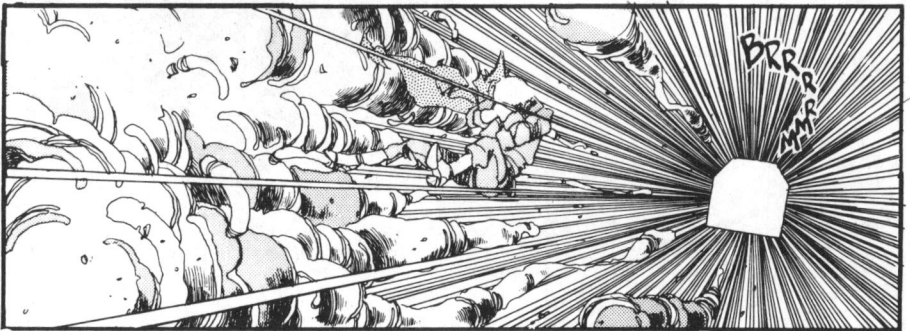

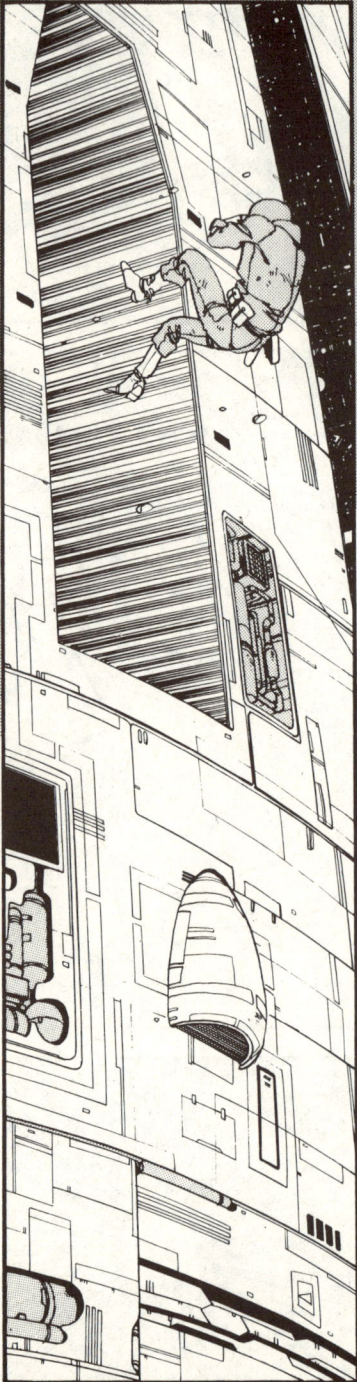

PSSH

Approach Eight: Nagoshi, Part 2

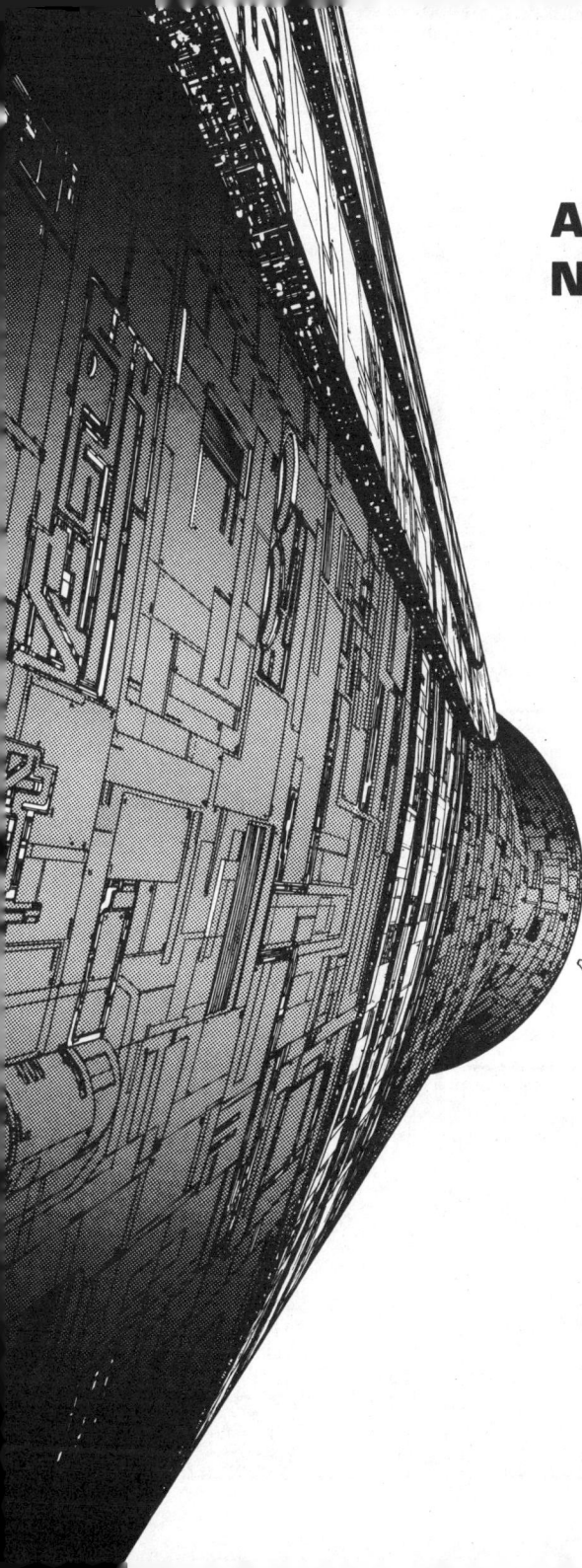

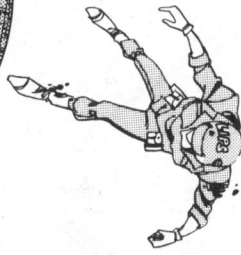

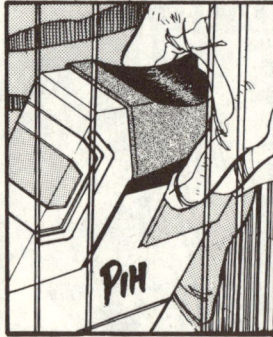

CHIK

WELL. MY WRIST IS DISLOCATED...

ZHHH

ZHHH

ZHHH

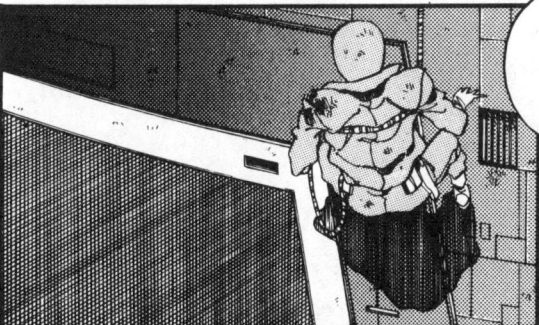

THAT'S GREAT.

SHAA!

wunK

UNGH!

MY BODY IS WOUNDED AND BATTERED...

IT'S THE MOST DESPERATE HOUR OF MY BATTLE...

OH, WHAT WILL HAPPEN TO OUR HERO NOW?

QUESTION IS...HOW FAR DID I DROP?

YO. ROBERT!

DAMN!

WOOPS.

NOW WHAT--?

HYAHH!!

VOOM

bying

PEEE

NOT EVEN *CLOSE!*

BAM

HUHH!!

WAP

WHUMP

BYING

BLAP!

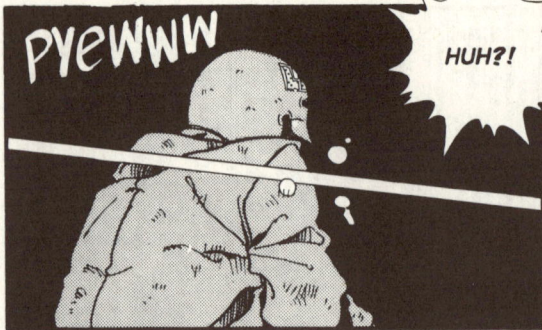

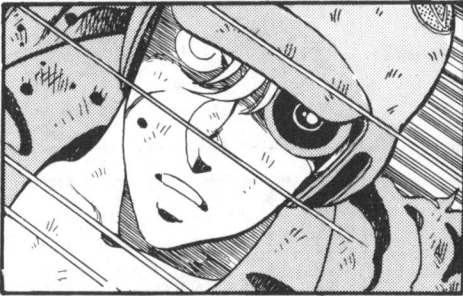

WUMP

B'NOON!!

SHIT!

TOO...
DAMN...
PERSIST...

SQUELCH

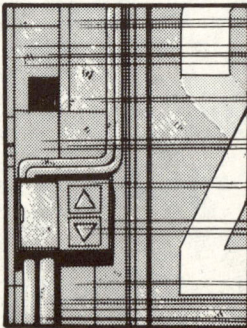

UH
OH.

WELL, NOW HERE'S A CONVENIENT SURPRISE.

BIP

PEEEEE

PEEEEE

!!

NOW, CAN IT REALLY BE...

KSSH

...THAT THIS SWITCH...

YEAH.
IT
CAN.

!!

BYING

TOO BAD THEY DON'T MAKE BEAM-CANNONS FOR USE IN THE SHOWER.

GOOD TIMING.

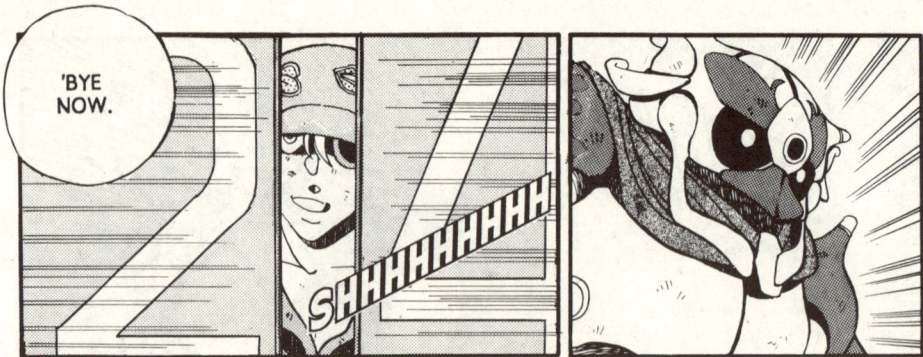

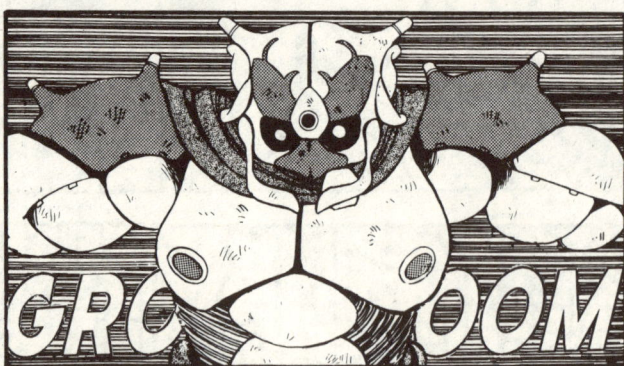

WELL, THAT'S *SOMETHING* TO BE PROUD OF.

BLOW

S.LAP!

SHHHHHHHHHH

GYUUUNN

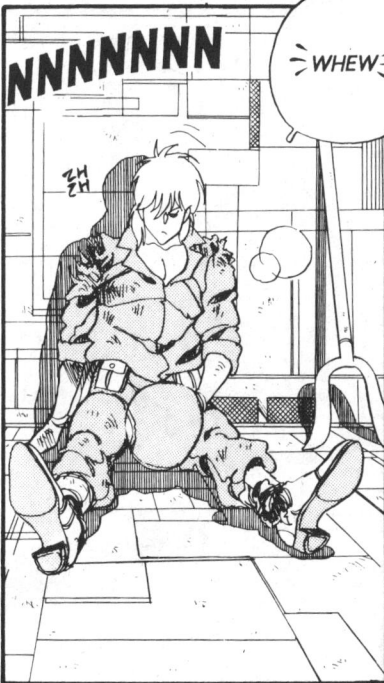

NNNNNNN

ZH ZH

WHEW

NNNNNNN

ONE ARM... JUST ABOUT GONE...

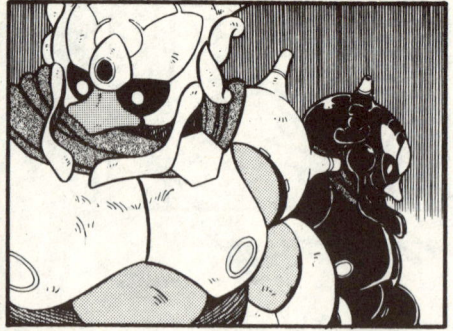

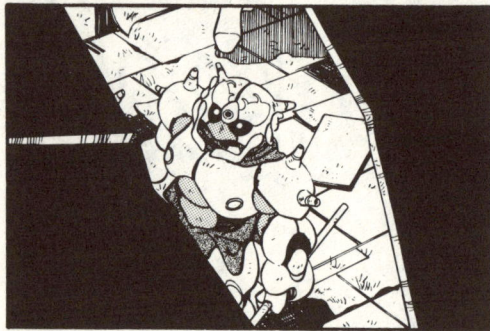

DON'T FIND
ME YET...
A COUPLE
MINUTES...

...TIME TO
CONNECT
THIS
WIRE...

NOT
YET.

OKAY.

HEY.
I GOT
SOMETHING
FOR
YOU.

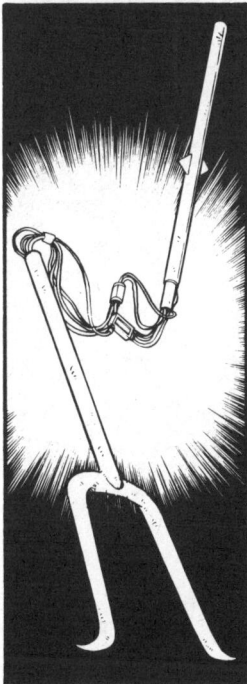

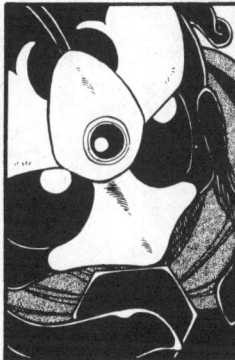

DINK

ZAK!

BAGOOM

SORRY, GUYS.

KREEE
KREEE
KREEE

KREE

I'VE BEEN ISSUED SUCH LOUSY WEAPONS--I'VE HAD TO GET GOOD AT *CUSTOMIZING* THEM.

KREE

KREE

NOW...

WHAT FLOOR IS THE MAIN COMPUTER ON?

IT SHOULD BE AS FAR FROM THE ENGINE AS POSSIBLE.

KREE

KREE

KREE

WHICH WOULD PUT IT IN THIS STATUE'S *HEAD.*

AND THAT'S A *LONG* WAY.

IF YOU'RE STILL ALIVE, ROBERT... I'M SORRY ABOUT THIS.

BUT I DON'T HAVE TIME FOR ANY RESCUES.

KREE

KREE

KREE

MAYBE NO TIME...

BEFORE *I* BUY IT, TOO.

126

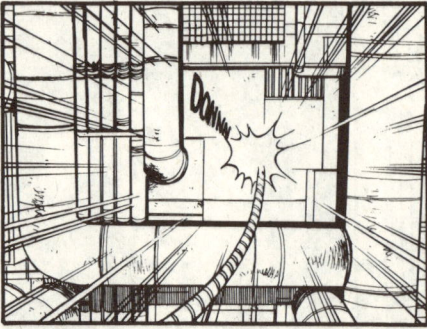

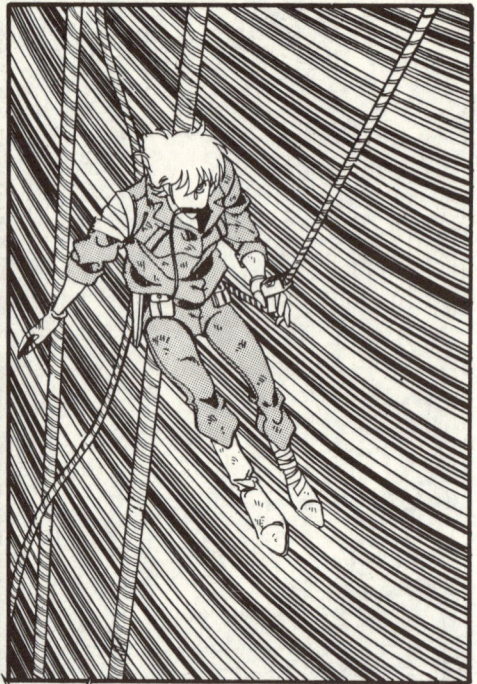

UHH!

KA-CHANK

DAMN... PAIN.

ZHEE
ZHEE
ZHEE

WISH THEY WERE *ALWAYS* THIS HOSPITABLE.

HMM...

WHAT--

WHOA!!

YOW!

AUGH!

PYEW

ZOOK

OOK

ZHA?

ZOOK

DAMN.

HELL OF A WAY TO ATTACK.

NO CLASS.

OH--

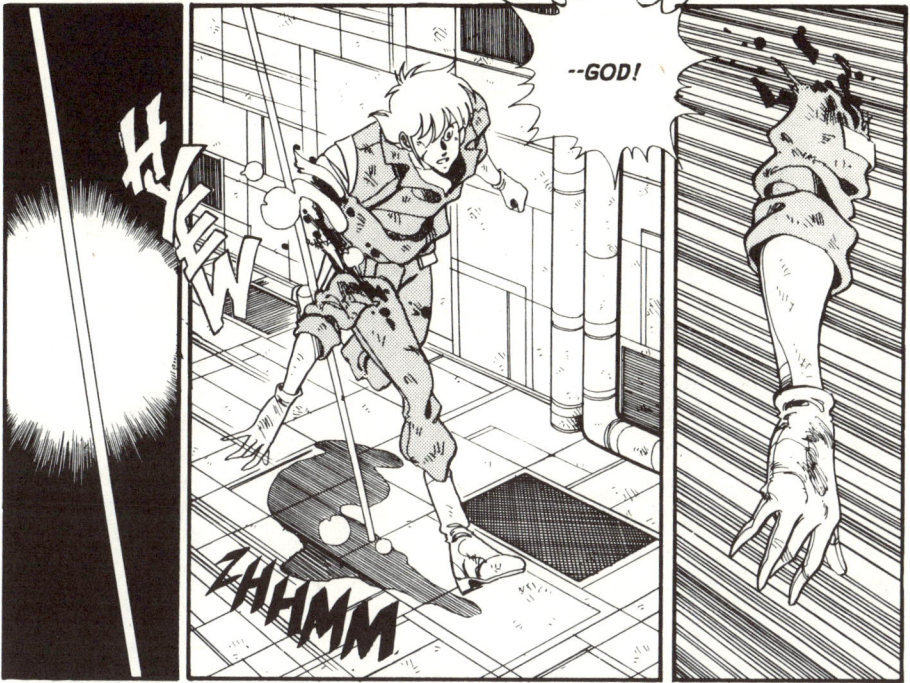

NO!!

BAMP

SH
SH
SH

KLONG

LIPS

NOW!

BONG

TONK

133

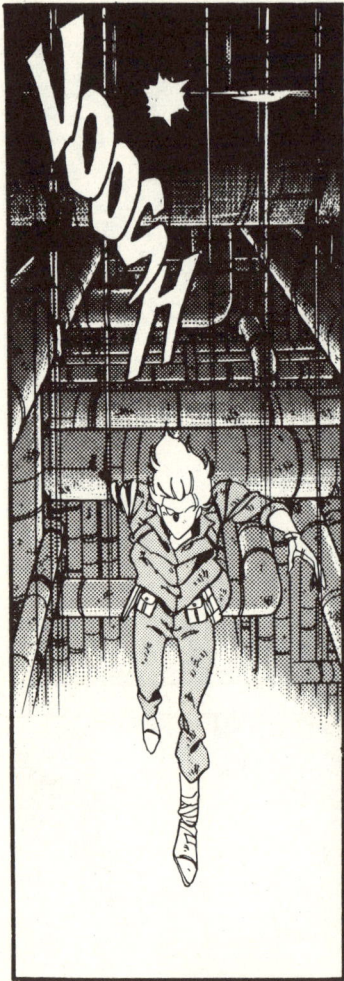

Approach Eight: Nagoshi, Part 3

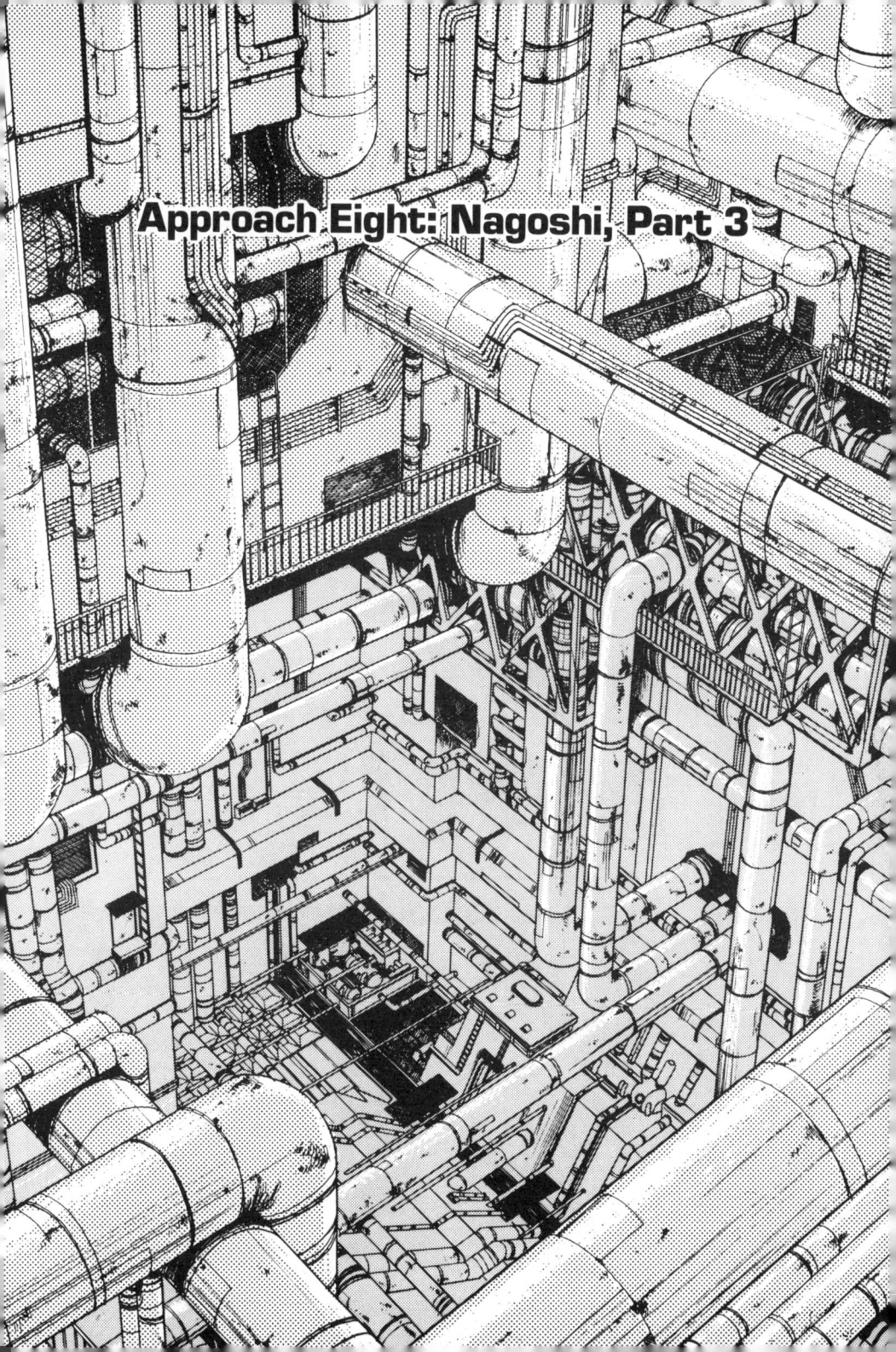

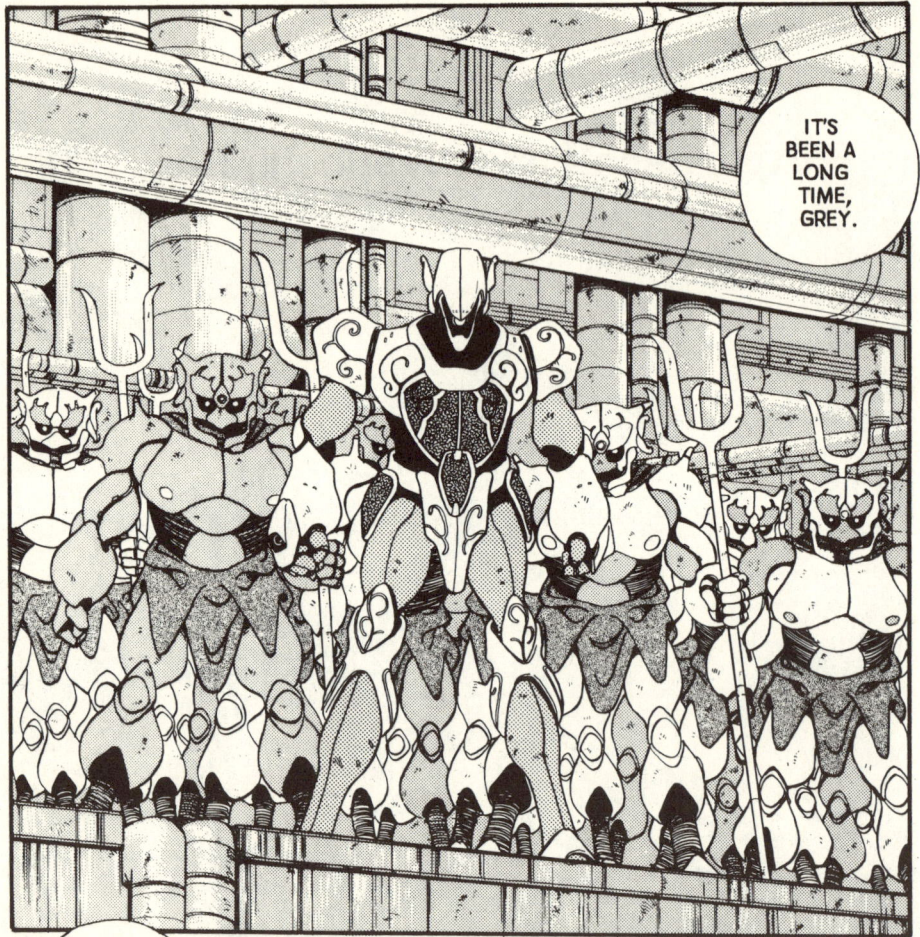

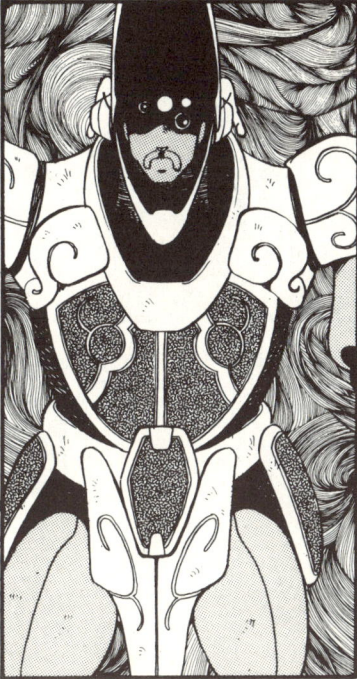

YOU'RE A *HALFLING* NOW... RED.

YEAH. AFTER MY LAND-CARRIER WAS ACED.

WELL. I DO HOPE THE *RESISTANCE* IS KEEPING YOU HAPPY.

YOU'LL UNDERSTAND SOON TOO, GREY.

I DON'T WANT TO.

AND
I
JUST...
DON'T...

...CARE...

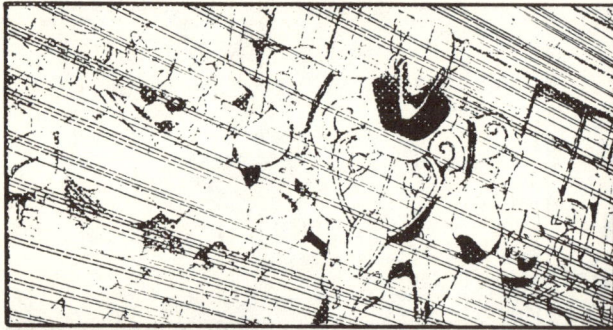

CARDIAC
PUMP
IS
OPERATING.

EKG,
NORMAL...

EEG,
NORMAL...

138

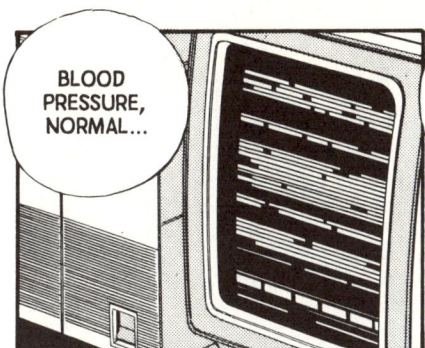

139

140

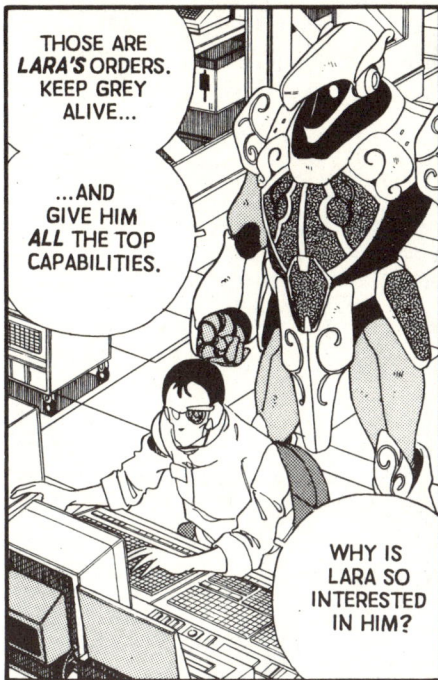

THOSE ARE *LARA'S* ORDERS. KEEP GREY ALIVE...

...AND GIVE HIM *ALL* THE TOP CAPABILITIES.

WHY IS LARA SO INTERESTED IN HIM?

MAYBE...GREY'S THE ONE WHO CAN GO UP AGAINST *BIG MAMA.*

WELL...IT'S TRUE THAT HE'S THE ONLY ATTACKER EVER TO REACH THE CORE OF NAGOSHI.

TENACITY, I SUPPOSE.

NO. ANGER.

ANGER? ABOUT WHAT?

ABOUT EVERYTHING.

141

ABOUT THE FILTHY TOWN HE WAS BORN IN...

...THE LOUSY FOOD THEY GOT.

STARE AND THEN LOOK AWAY SORRY"!

...TILL WE DIE.

I'D HATE TO THINK YOU WERE DOING SOMETHING YOU DIDN'T FEEL LIKE.

WE'RE DIFFERENT FROM YOU "PEOPLE" WE'RE ANOTHER BREED UNDER...

AND DO YOU FOR...

SURE THING.

ABOUT THE ARROGANCE OF THE *TROOPERS*...

AND THE FACT THAT YOU HAVE TO *JOIN* THE TROOPERS TO BECOME A *CITIZEN*...

KILLING OTHER POOR BASTARDS WHO WANT TO BE CITIZENS...

WHILE THE *RESISTANCE* INTERFERES.

THAT YOU HAVE TO STRUGGLE YOUR WAY UP TO *CLASS A*... THAT YOU DO THAT BY KILLING...

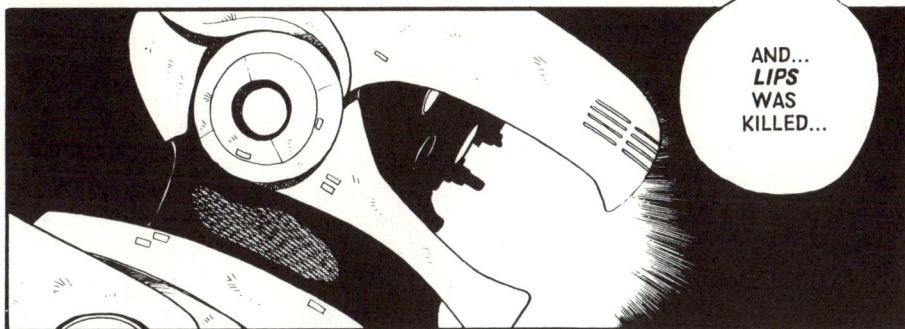

KASUGA-- DEMON SQUAD 24--

--HAVE YOU FOUND THE BODY OF THE HALFLING WHO PILOTED THE ATTACKER'S KUBANDA?

NO CONFIRMATION YET, SIR.

SHIT. EVERY 30 SECONDS THE SAME DAMN QUES--

IVAN FOUND THIS ON THE UPPER LEVEL.

CAPTAIN.

THE HALFLING'S HAND?

I DON'T THINK IT'S HIS HEAD.

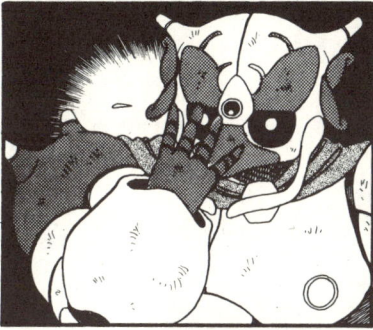

I CAN'T LAST MUCH LONGER IN THIS BODY, GREY.

GO FETCH RAMOS OF SERVICE CREW C.

ROGER, SIR!

HEY, YOU! *ION!*

WHAT'S HIS NAME? UH...*GREY.* YEAH.

I HEARD RED WAS HIS SUPERIOR WHEN THEY WERE BOTH TROOPERS.

OKAY. THAT EXPLAINS WHY THEY GAVE HIM THE HALFLING TREATMENT.

SO... GREY'S BECOME A HALFLING.

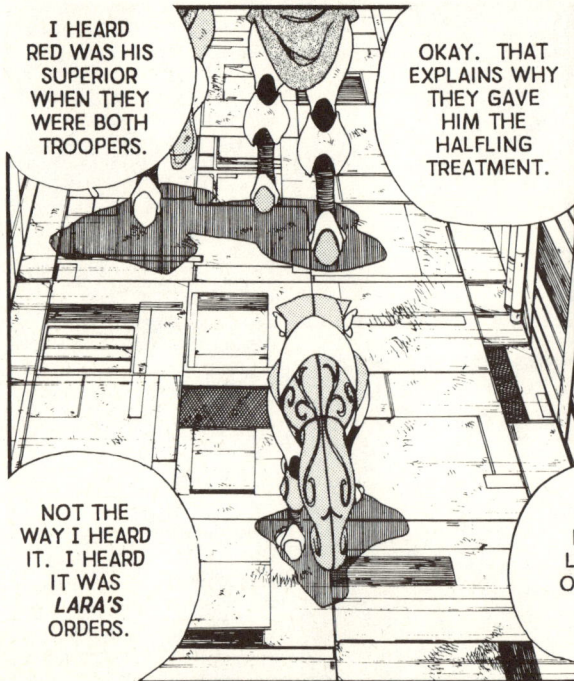

NOT THE WAY I HEARD IT. I HEARD IT WAS *LARA'S* ORDERS.

HMM. LARA'S ORDERS.

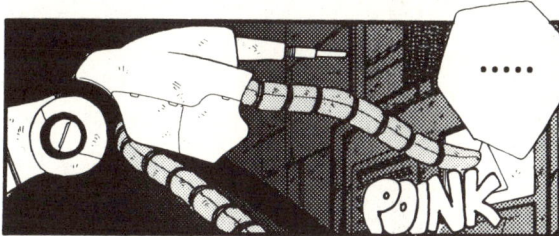

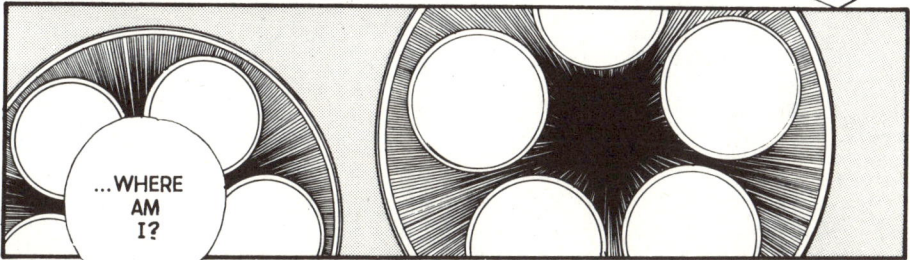

YOU FINALLY AWAKE?

UH...

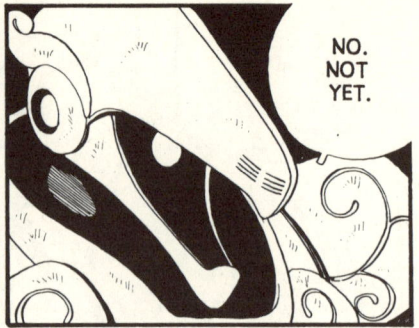

NO. NOT YET.

WH...

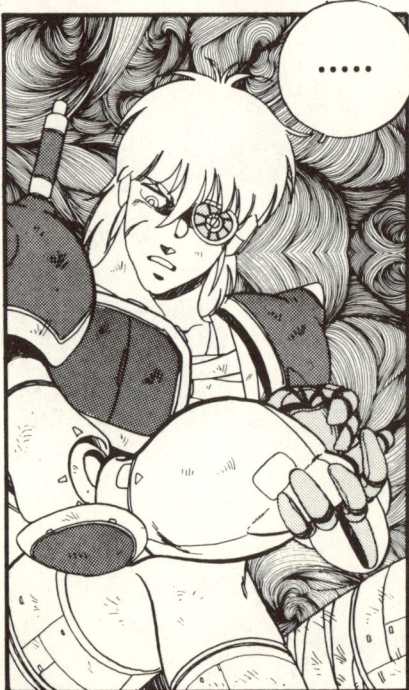

· · · · ·

WHAT IS THIS?

WE GAVE YOU A HALFLING OPERATION, GREY.

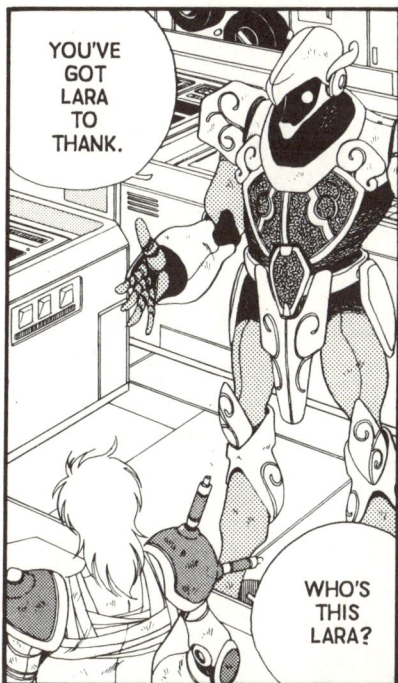

IT DOESN'T LOOK GOOD.

MY LIFE MAY END A BIT SOONER THAN I THOUGHT.

WELL, THEN, IF THAT'S THE CASE...

I HAVE ONE LAST RESORT.

KA! TUMP

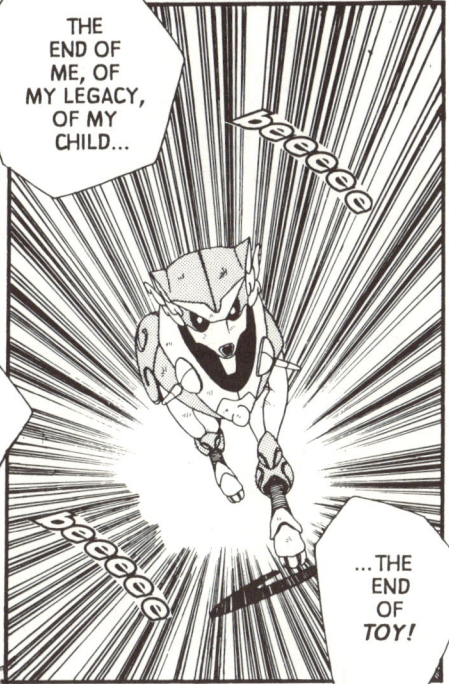

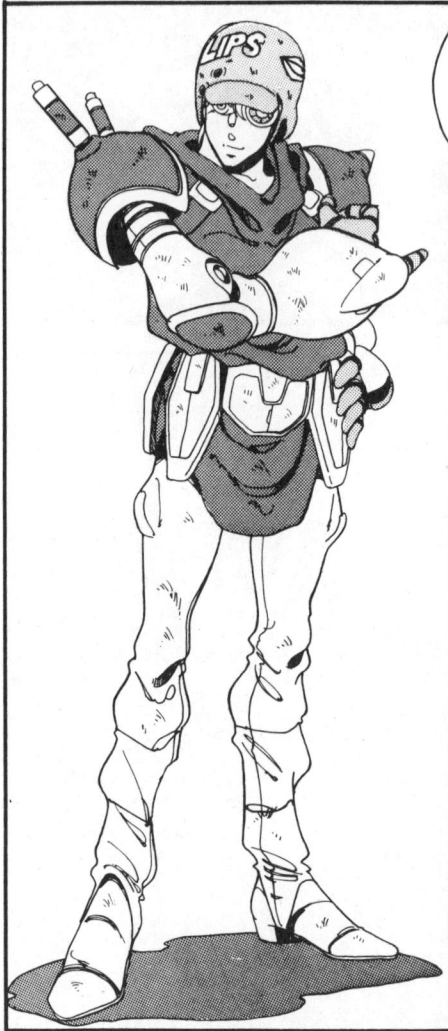

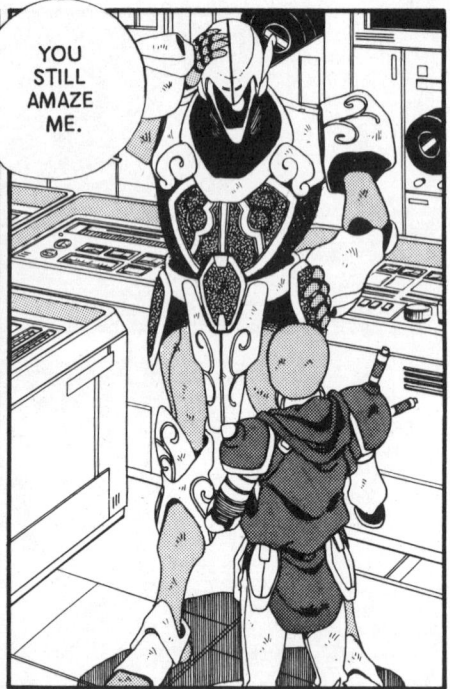

YOU STILL AMAZE ME.

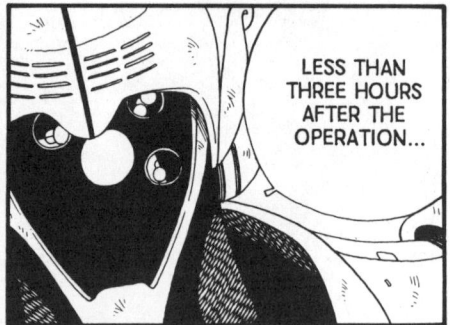

LESS THAN THREE HOURS AFTER THE OPERATION...

A NORMAL MAN WOULDN'T EVEN BE ABLE TO CRAWL OUT OF *BED.*

SINCE WHEN IS *DEATH* A NORMAL MAN?

TOOK ME A **WEEK** BEFORE I COULD WALK.

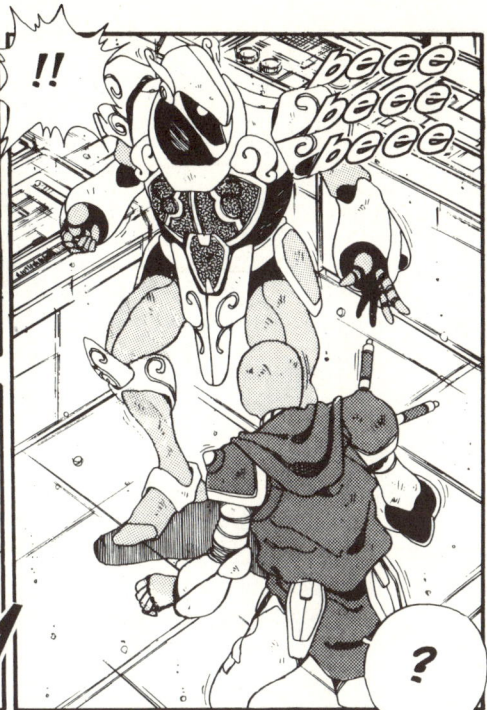

beee
beee
beee

!!

?

YOU'RE JUST TOO **COOL** TO--

BRRRMMM

WHAT IS IT, CONTROL?

.....

BIK

AN ION!

AN ION TRIGGERED AN EXPLOSION IN THE MASTER COMPUTER--

--WE'RE LOSING ALL CONTROL.

I REPEAT--AN ION TRIGGERED AN EXPLOSION IN THE MASTER COMPUTER...

AN "ION"?

A KIND OF DOLL. MODELED AFTER SOME ANIMAL CALLED A "DOG."

RRRRMMM

THE MASTER COMP MUST'VE BEEN ICED.

ROBERT...

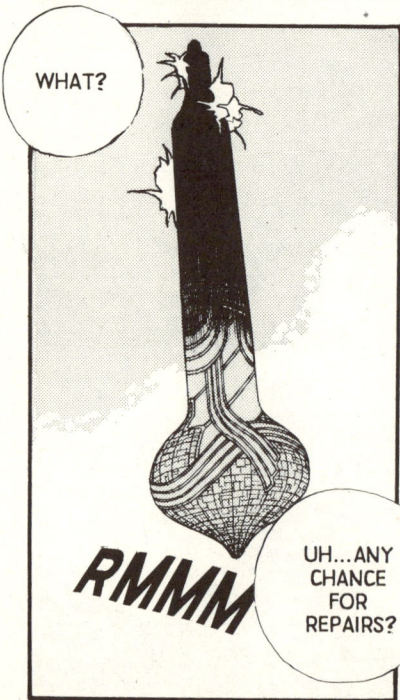

WHAT?

UH...ANY CHANCE FOR REPAIRS?

RMMM

NIX. THE SUB-COMP CAN COVER FOR A WHILE. BUT THIS BASE...

...IT'S JUST TOO DAMN BIG FOR A SUB-COMP.

RRM RRM

RRM

I DON'T KNOW IF WE'LL EVEN BE ABLE TO MAKE A SAFE LANDING.

154

YOU SHOULD ESCAPE WHILE YOU CAN, GREY.

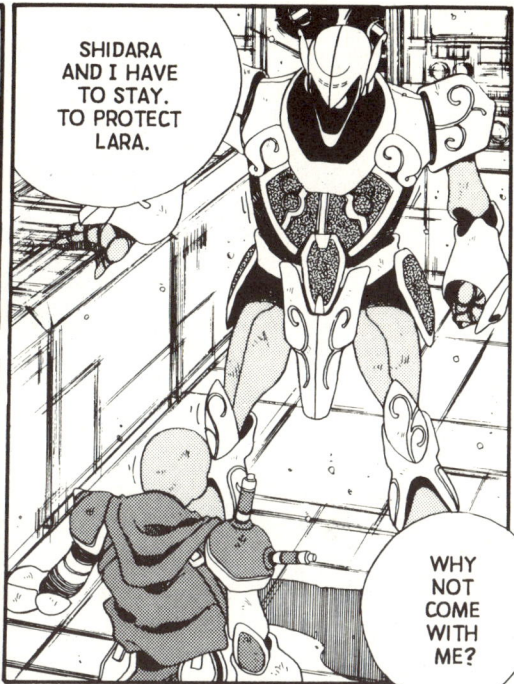

SHIDARA AND I HAVE TO STAY. TO PROTECT LARA.

WHY NOT COME WITH ME?

HOW ABOUT YOU?

I DON'T WANT TO HAVE TO FIGHT YOU, RED.

I KNOW. I DON'T WANT TO FIGHT YOU EITHER.

BUT NAGOSHI MUST DESTROY BIG MAMA AND HER CITY!

ZWOOM

WHY, RED?

WHY STICK WITH NAGOSHI?!

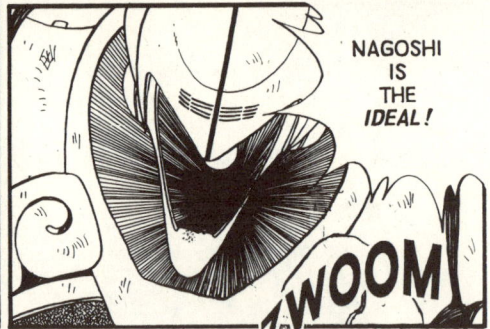

NAGOSHI IS THE *IDEAL!*

ZWOOM

THE IDEAL?

CHANK

ONLY FOR THE CHOSEN *FEW,* RED!

DAMN IT, IT'S JUST LIKE THE *CITY!*

NO!!

156

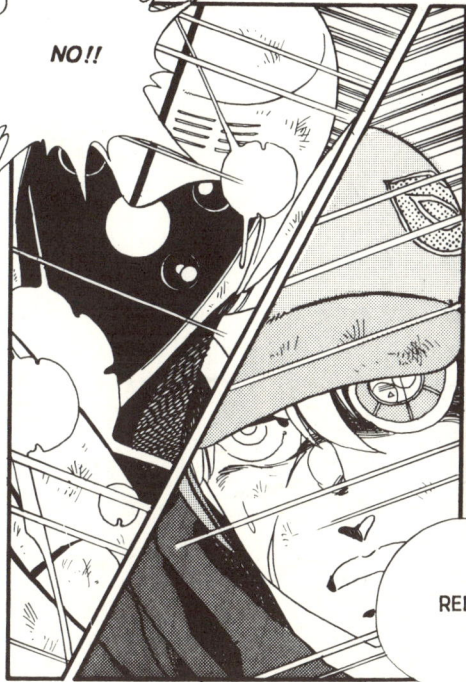

NAGOSHI... CITY...

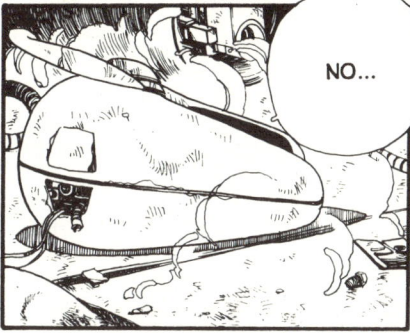

NO...

NAGOSHI... IDEAL...

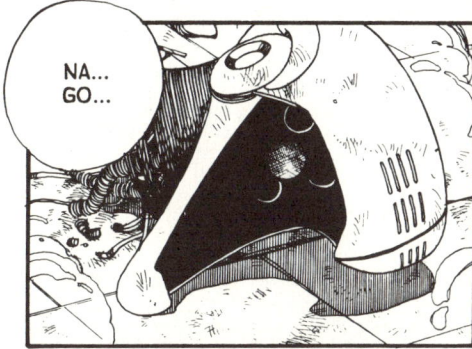

NA... GO...

BASTARDS. BRAINWASHED...

RRMM

BA KOOM

BOOOM

SUB-COMP HAS LOST CONTROL.

ENGINE 12 IS NOW COMPLETELY DOWN.

ALL SECTIONS DESTROYED ON LEVEL 133.

SECTIONS 108, 109, ON LEVEL 132 DESTROYED.

BLAHM

RRRRRRRR

ENGINE 5... DOWN.

ENGINES 2 AND 3 ARE FAILING.

ALL PERSONNEL EVACUATE NOW.

FWSHHH

LARA! THIS WAY!

I WON'T LET YOU!

KLANG

HAH!!

GRRROOOMM

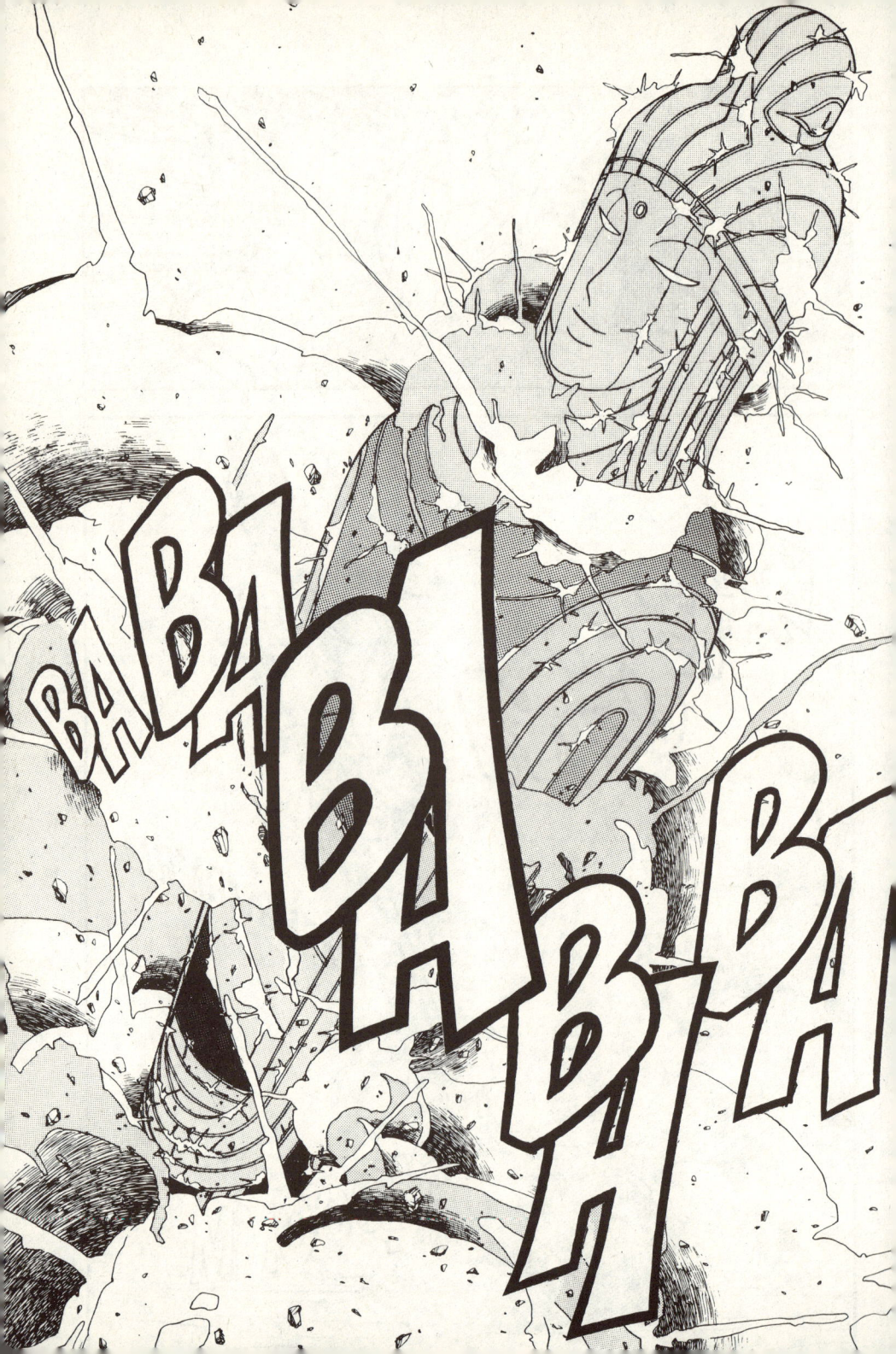

Approach Nine: Lara

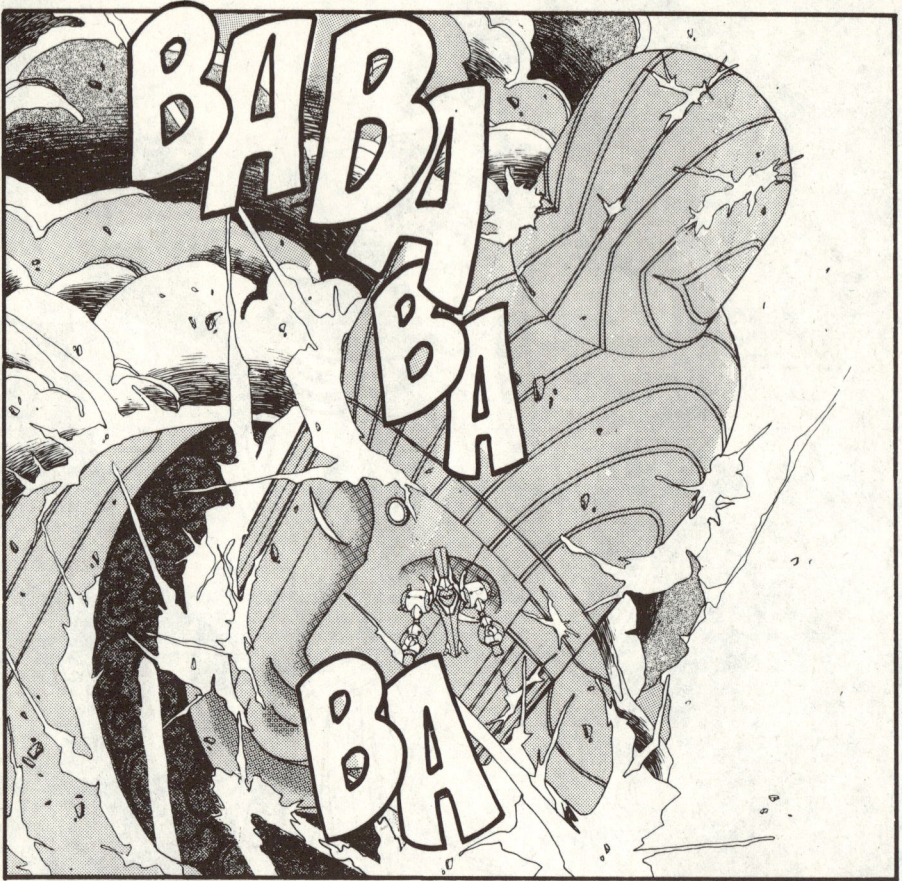

VROW

VMMMMMMM

SHIDARA...

...AND GREY.

BM BM BM BM

VROW

PYEW!

UHH!

I WON'T LET YOU ESCAPE!

NO KIDDING!

VROOO

...THAT I'M *ESCAPING?!*

BLOM!

BUT WHO SAYS...

NOW!!

KLASH

OH!!

DAMN YOU...

QUEEEEEE

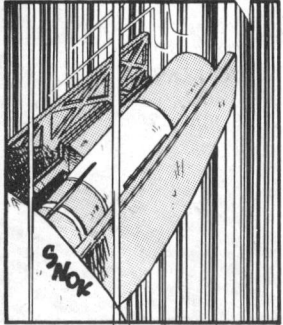

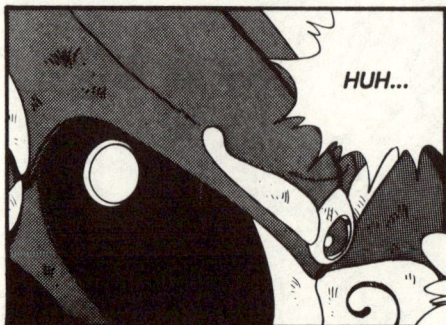

THE CITY.

GREY, SHIDARA AND I...

WE'RE ALL TOGETHER, AREN'T WE?

HMPH.

I THOUGHT YOU WERE JUST ANOTHER PRETTY FACE. BUT YOU'RE A PRETTY *TALKER*, TOO.

I WON'T ASK YOU TO TRUST ME. BUT YOU CAN *USE* ME, CAN YOU NOT?

THE THREE OF US CAN COOPERATE... AT LEAST ON *THOSE* TERMS.

AM I CORRECT, SHIDARA? GREY?

DO YOU REMEMBER WHEN ONE OF YOUR SCOUTING PLANES ACED A PROTOTYPE *OHM?*

WHAT ARE YOU TALKING ABOUT?

WAS THIS WHEN WE DESTROYED THE BATTALION FROM TOWN 91?

THAT'S WHEN THEY DIED. *LEE* AND... *NOVA.*

LEE? THE LEE WHO BELONGED TO SHIDARA?

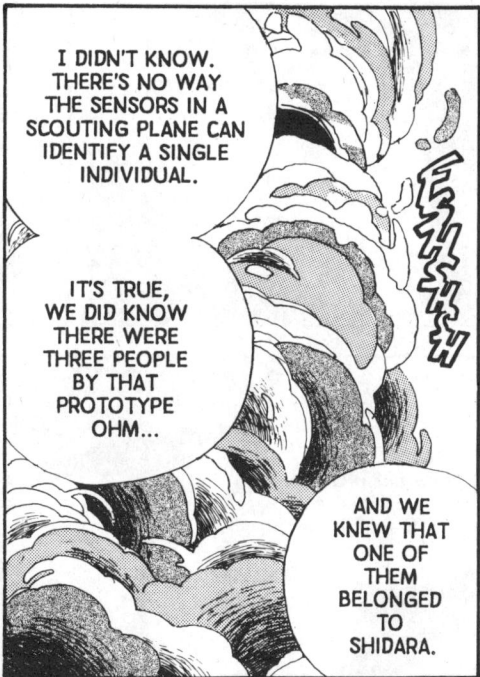

I DIDN'T KNOW. THERE'S NO WAY THE SENSORS IN A SCOUTING PLANE CAN IDENTIFY A SINGLE INDIVIDUAL.

IT'S TRUE, WE DID KNOW THERE WERE THREE PEOPLE BY THAT PROTOTYPE OHM...

AND WE KNEW THAT ONE OF THEM BELONGED TO SHIDARA.

BUT HOW COULD WE KNOW THAT THE OTHER TWO WEREN'T *TROOPERS* FROM 91?

WHENEVER NAGOSHI FIRES A *KRAG-SHOT,* NEARLY ALL ITS DEFENSES GO TEMPORARILY DOWN, SO...

I GUESS... EVEN IF I'D KNOWN IT WAS LEE...I WOULDN'T HAVE HESITATED.

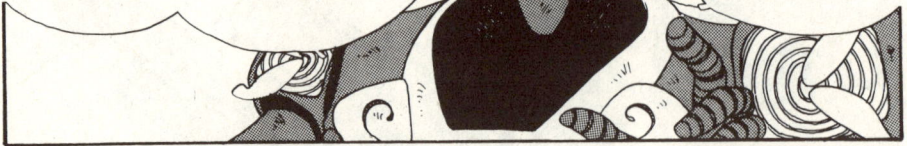

WHY DID YOU BRAINWASH *RED?*

I NEVER GAVE ANY SUCH ORDER!

SHIDARA, DID YOU--?

BRAIN-WASH--?

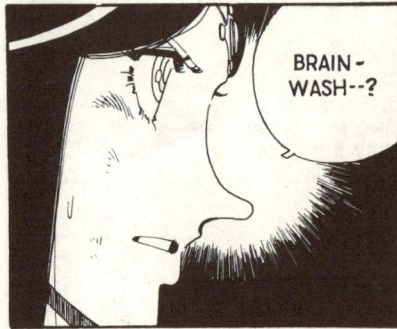

HE WAS SO STUBBORN...

IF I HADN'T DONE IT, NAGOSHI WOULD HAVE BEEN DESTROYED EVEN EARLIER.

HE WOULD HAVE JOINED WITH GREY...

NAGOSHI GOT ACED ANYWAY, DIDN'T IT?

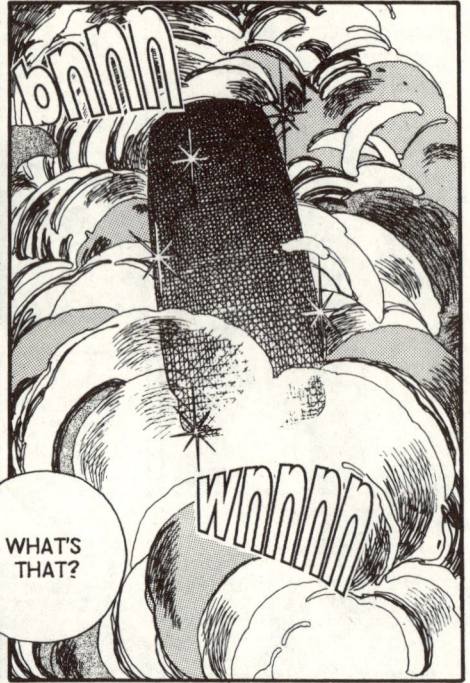

WHAT DO WE DO, SHIDARA?

WHAT CAN WE DO...BUT FIGHT?

THREE OF US, AGAINST SUCH A SHIP...

BNNN

WNNN

IT'S TOO *RECKLESS!*

YOU WITH ME, SHIDARA?

MIGHT AS WELL BE.

LARA-- YOU REMAIN *HERE!*

GREY-- MOUNT LARA'S *GARUDA!*

BA-FOOD

NO! I'M COMING!

A GARUDA WILL CARRY *TWO!*

NO TIME TO *WASTE,* GREY!

I'M NOT... WASTING TIME.

YOU'RE TOO DAMN SLOW IN THOSE CLOTHES.

Ba-FOOO

COULD YOU KEEP YOUR MIND ON THE BATTLE IF I TOOK THEM OFF?

I'M READY-- LET'S GO!

SURE OF YOURSELF, MM?

.....

WHAT HAVE I BEEN DOING SO FAR?

VWAH!

THE BANTER CAN WAIT, GREY!

COVER ME!

I'M GOING IN FOR THEIR MAIN COMPUTER!

HYAHHH!!

I DON'T THINK YOU'RE GETTING IN, OLD MAN!

DAMN!!

184

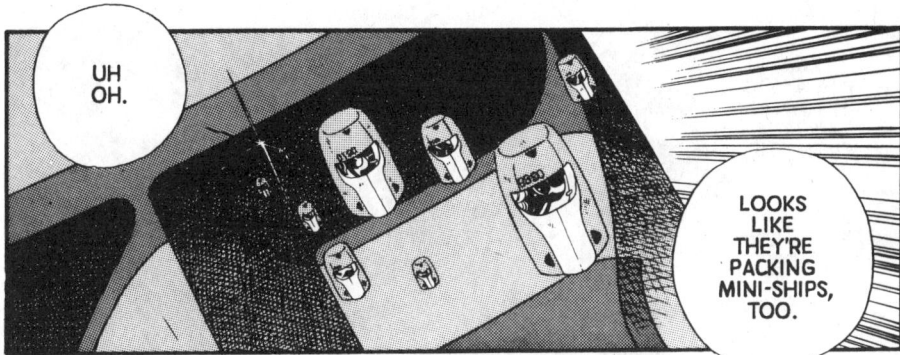

UH OH.

LOOKS LIKE THEY'RE PACKING MINI-SHIPS, TOO.

YOU KIDDING?

I'M BUSY ENOUGH JUST DANCING WITH THESE MINI-PLANES.

I MEAN A *KRAG-SHOT!!*

HIT THE *LAUNCH-BAY,* GREY!

CAN THIS GARUDA DO THAT?

IN THEORY, AT LEAST.

WELL, THAT'S COMFORTING.

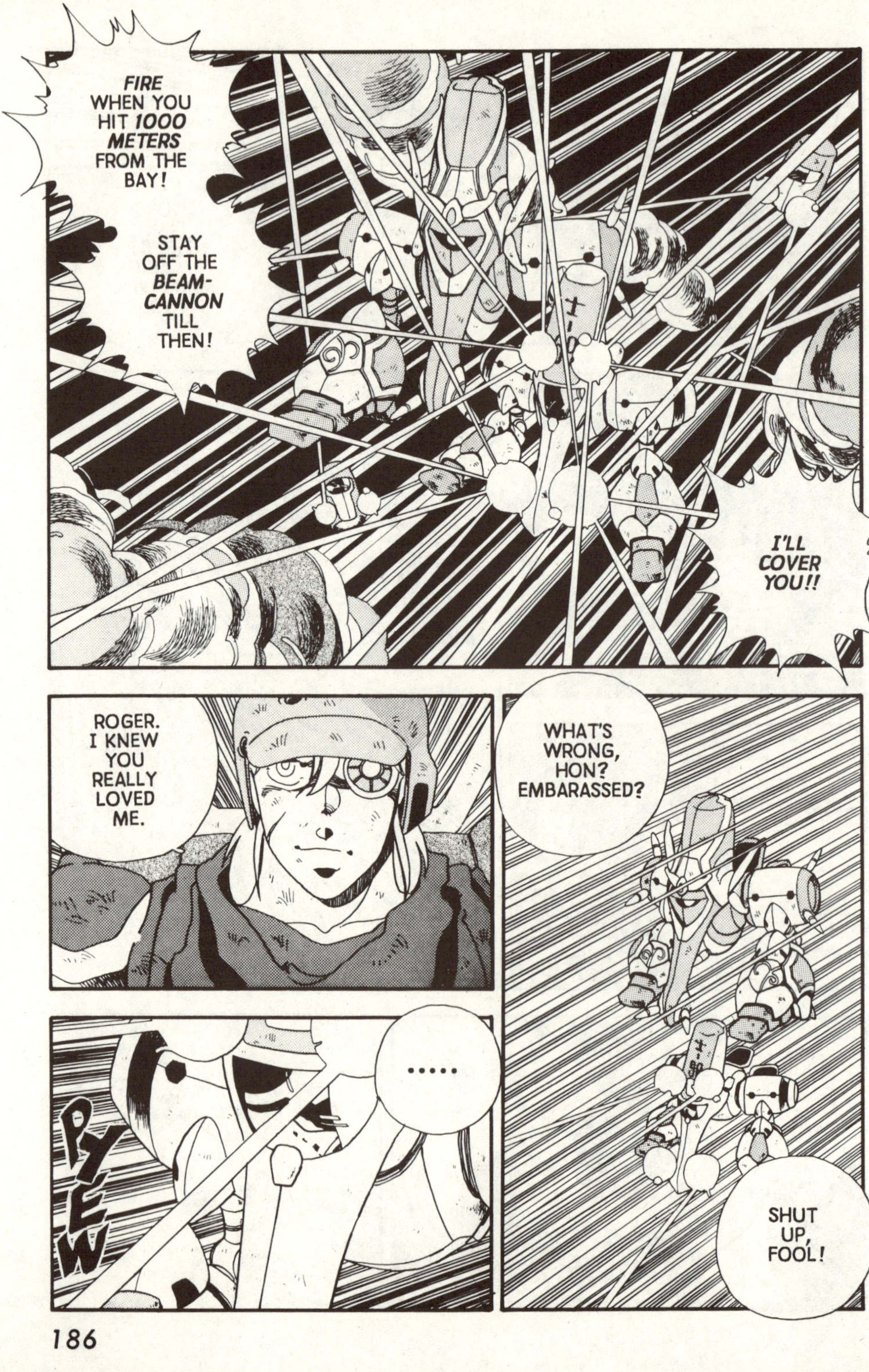
FIRE WHEN YOU HIT 1000 METERS FROM THE BAY!
STAY OFF THE BEAM-CANNON TILL THEN!
I'LL COVER YOU!!
ROGER. I KNEW YOU REALLY LOVED ME.
WHAT'S WRONG, HON? EMBARASSED?
......
PYEW
SHUT UP, FOOL!

HMPH. NO SENSE OF HUMOR.

THAT'S NATURAL...

A DOLL?

SHIDARA ISN'T A HALFLING, BUT A DOLL.

BUT I HEARD HE WAS A CLASS-B TROOPER.

HE WAS. FROM TOWN 424. BUT THEN THE TOWN'S *LITTLE MAMA* WENT OUT OF CONTROL.

SHIDARA HAD JUST COME BACK FROM A BATTLE THEATER THE DAY BEFORE...

WHEN HE WAS KILLED BY THE LITTLE MAMA.

JUST BEFORE BRAIN-DEATH, HIS ENTIRE MEMORY WAS REMOVED, AND INPUT INTO AN ELECTRONIC BRAIN, WHICH IN TURN WAS INSTALLED IN A DOLL. THAT'S THE SHIDARA YOU KNOW.

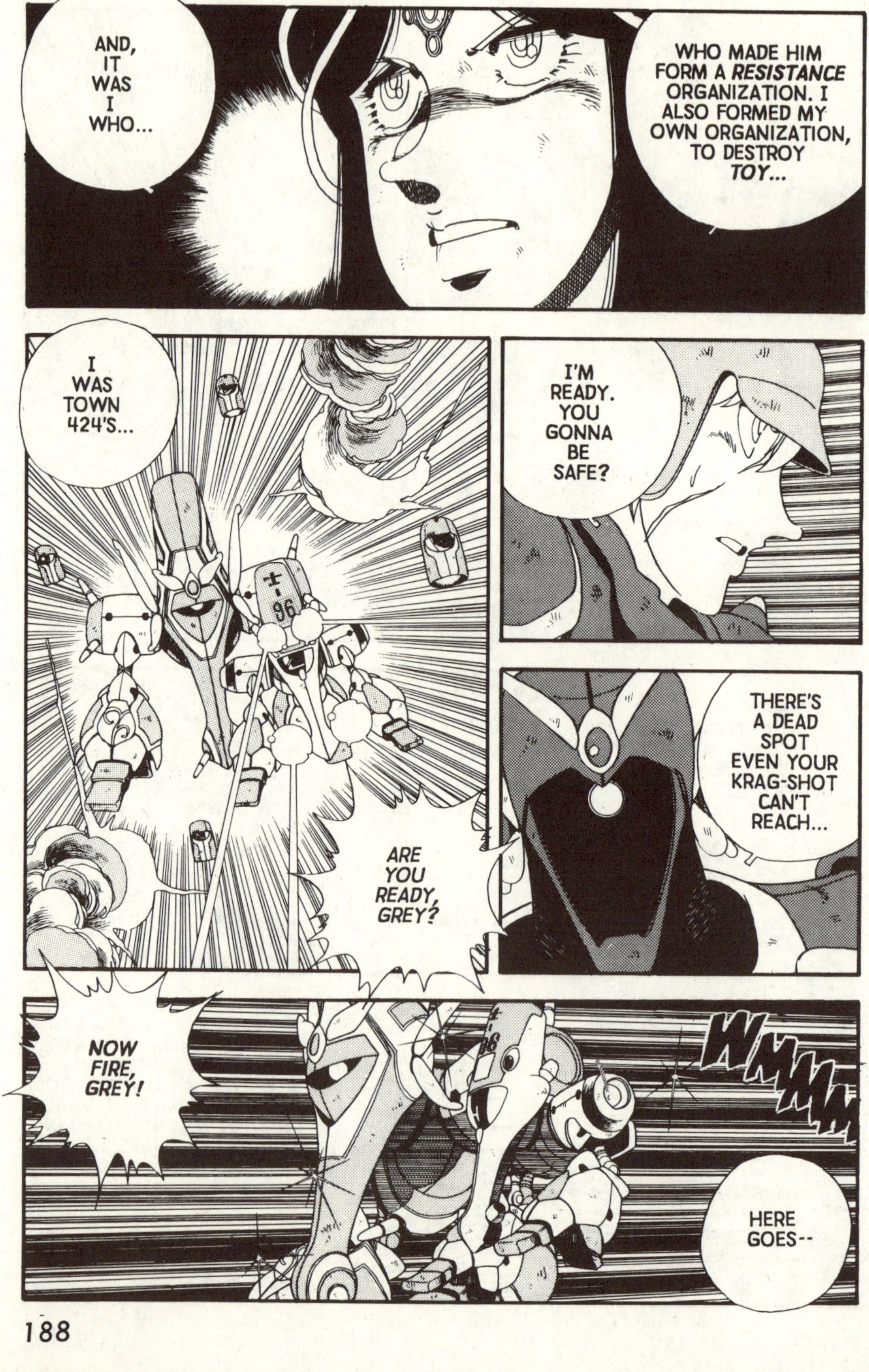
AND, IT WAS I WHO...
WHO MADE HIM FORM A *RESISTANCE* ORGANIZATION. I ALSO FORMED MY OWN ORGANIZATION, TO DESTROY *TOY*...
I WAS TOWN 424'S...
I'M READY. YOU GONNA BE SAFE?
THERE'S A DEAD SPOT EVEN YOUR KRAG-SHOT CAN'T REACH...
ARE YOU READY, GREY?
NOW FIRE, GREY!
WMMMM
HERE GOES--

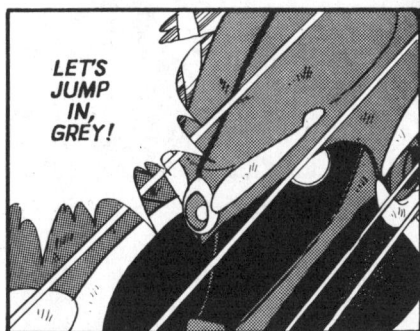

BUT HOW YOU GONNA FIND THE COMPUTER ROOM?

BOOM

WE'RE BOTH *HALFLINGS*, GREY...

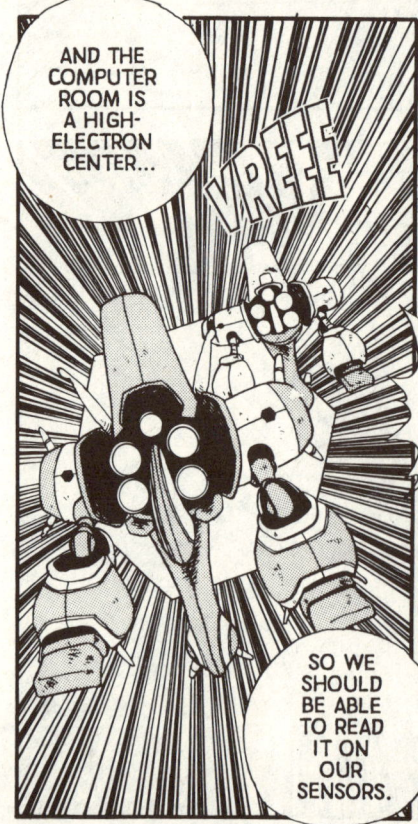

AND THE COMPUTER ROOM IS A HIGH-ELECTRON CENTER...

VREEE

SO WE SHOULD BE ABLE TO READ IT ON OUR SENSORS.

DOESN'T SHIDARA KNOW...

NO.

UP, GREY! UP!

VWAH

OUR *POWER'S* STILL DOWN!

IT TAKES ABOUT *FIVE MINUTES* TO RECHARGE!

ZHAP

UHH!

!!

PYEW

96

BOOM

PYEW

WHOMP

ZHAH

SHIDARA!
BEHIND
YOU!

beeeee

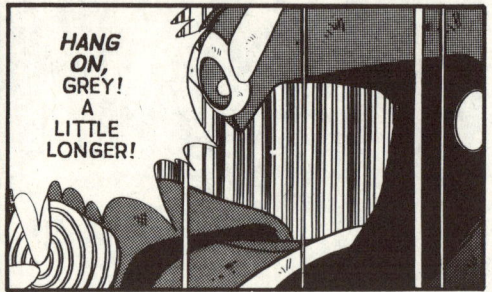

HANG
ON,
GREY! A
LITTLE
LONGER!

JUST
A LITTLE
MORE,
GREY!
THE
POWER'S
BUILDING!

YOU
TALK
LIKE
I'M
GIVING
UP.

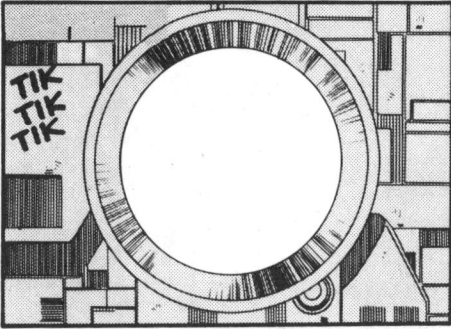

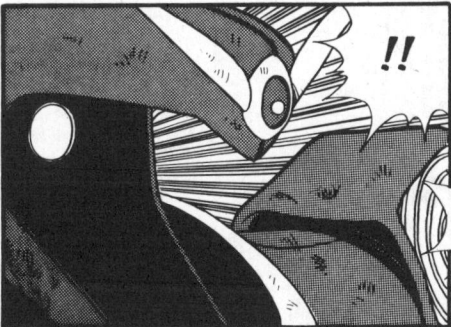

SHIDARA!!

A HEAT-ARROW...

BUH WISHHHH

POWER... 100 PERCENT!

SNIK SNIK SNIK

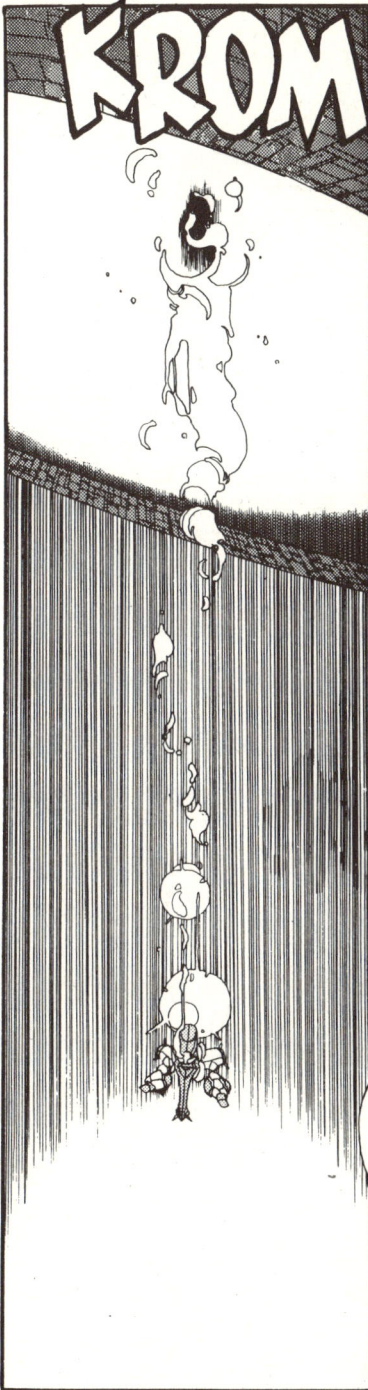

KROM

VROOO

KSHHHH

DID IT.

GREY...
GREY, I WAS...
DIDN'T GET SICK, DID YOU?
B-B-B-B-B-B-
I WAS... TOWN 424'S INFORMATION DOLL...
B-
I WAS "SURE."

Approach Ten:
The City, Part 1

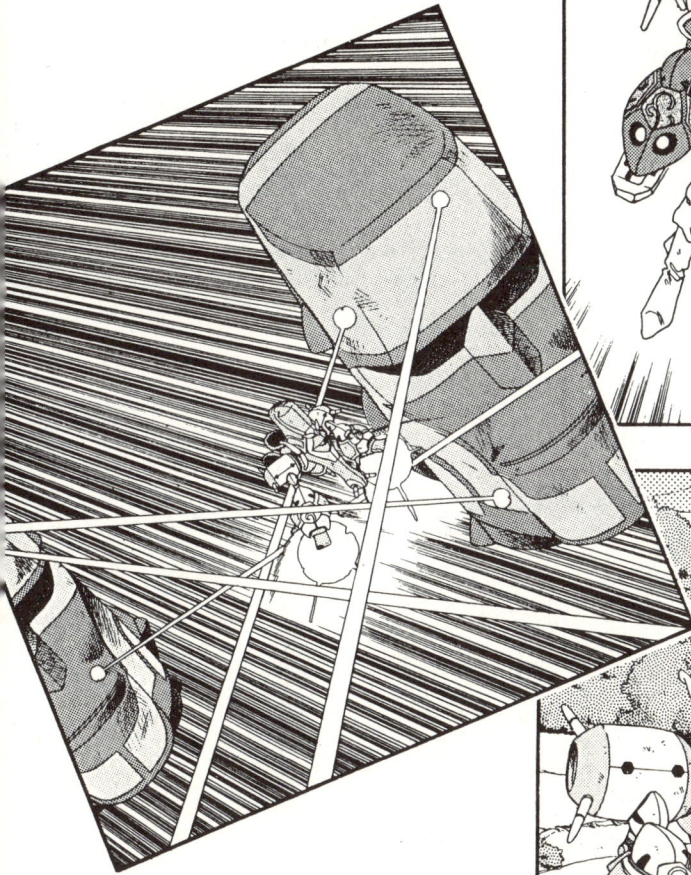

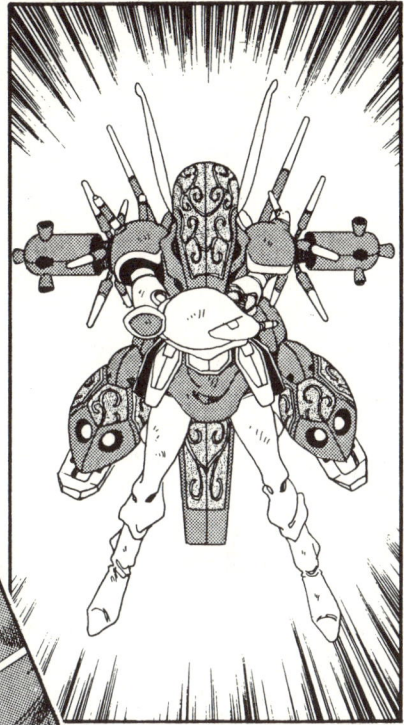

"SURE?"

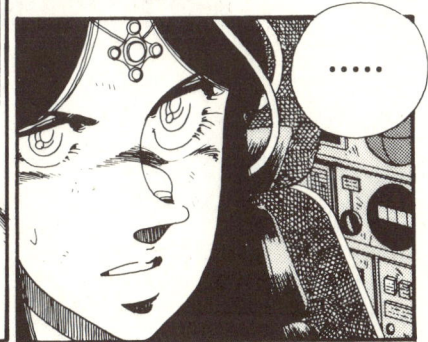

.....

WHAT
IS
IT?

YOU
DON'T
LOOK
LIKE
A
MACHINE.

WE GAVE YOU GOOD RADAR, DIDN'T WE?

VOWNN

.....

COMES IN HANDY, ANYWAY.

ROBERT MIGHT HAVE FORESEEN THE ENTIRE MATTER...

THUS, WHEN TOY FIRST CREATED THE CLASS SYSTEM...

...FROM THE DAY *TOY* FIRST ATTAINED CONSCIOUSNESS.

AND ITS TERMINALS, LITTLE MAMAS, BEGAN TO CONTROL EACH TOWN...

ROBERT PLACED A DUPLICATE OF HIMSELF AS A WATCHMAN FOR EACH LITTLE MAMA...

IF ANY LITTLE MAMA WENT OUT OF CONTROL, ITS *SURE* WOULD BE AWAKENED.

TO DESTROY TOY?

AND SO CREATED ME... *SURE.*

NO. TO HELP A *MAN* WHO MIGHT DESTROY TOY.

I'M A HALFLING. NOT A MAN.

BNNNNN BNNNNN

I AM A HALFLING, TOO...

BUT I'M DIFFERENT FROM YOU, GREY.

MY MIND IS A MACHINE.

YOURS IS HUMAN...

BEEP BEEP

BEEP

THOSE GUNSHIPS ARE FASTER THAN WE ARE.

YOU MIGHT BE ABLE TO SQUEEZE OFF ONE MORE SHOT...

YOU CAN'T USE THE KRAG-SHOT AGAIN.

WHY NOT?

BUT WE'LL FLY TO PIECES IN MID-AIR.

WE STILL HAVE...

...ONE OPTION, GREY.

IT'S HOPELESS, ISN'T IT?

NAGOSHI'S HIGHEST TECHNOLOGICAL ACHIEVEMENT... ISN'T THIS GARUDA.

IT'S *YOU*, GREY.

YOUR POWER IS *FAR* GREATER THAN THIS GARUDA'S.

THERE'S A FLIGHT-PACK YOU CAN USE, ALTHOUGH IT WAS CALIBRATED FOR SHIDARA.

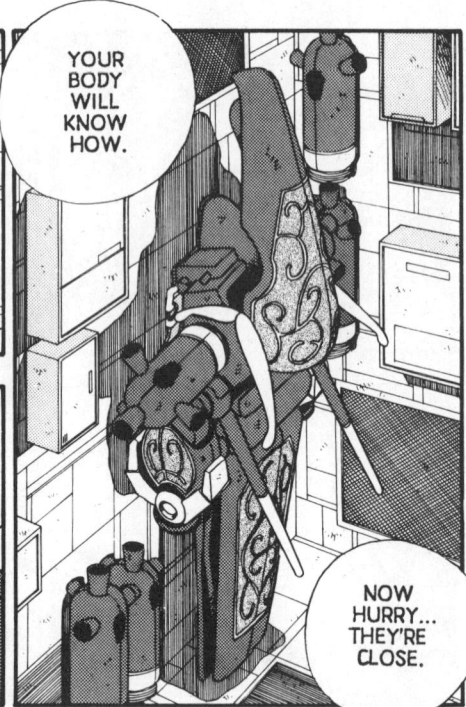

YOUR BODY WILL KNOW HOW.

NOW HURRY... THEY'RE CLOSE.

HOW DO I USE THIS FLIGHT-PACK?

I'LL LAUNCH YOU WHEN THEY REACH 3000 METERS. ALL RIGHT?

AND I'LL COVER YOU.

WHICH ONE DO I HIT FIRST?

THE *RIGHT.*

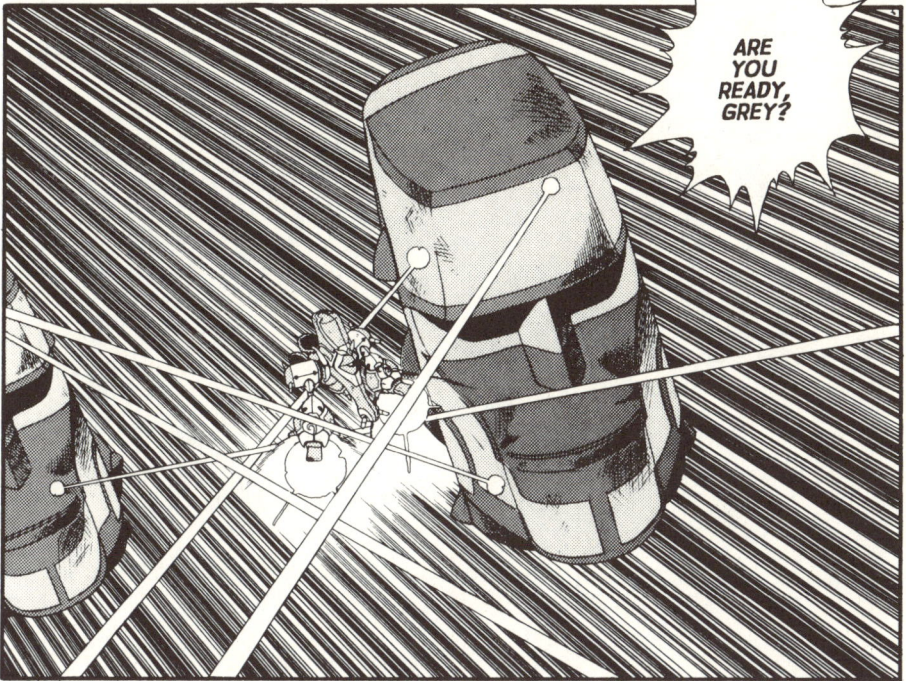

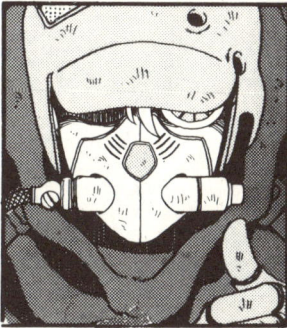

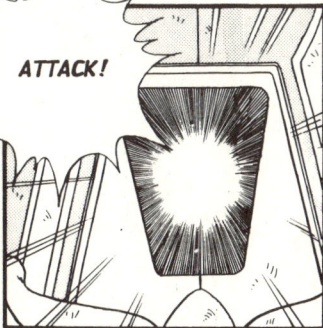

KLAK

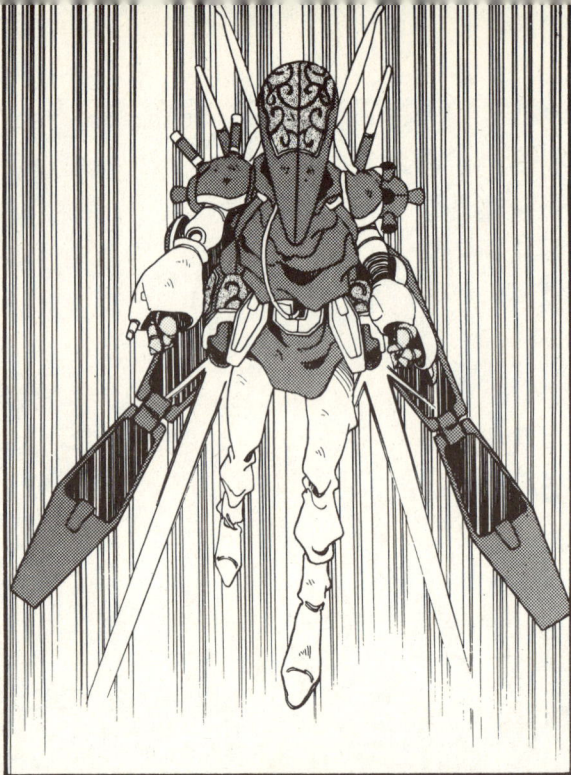

TRY TO SLIP UNDER THE GUNSHIP!

MINI-PLANES ATTACKING!

I'LL LEAVE 'EM TO YOU.

ROGER!

NOW!

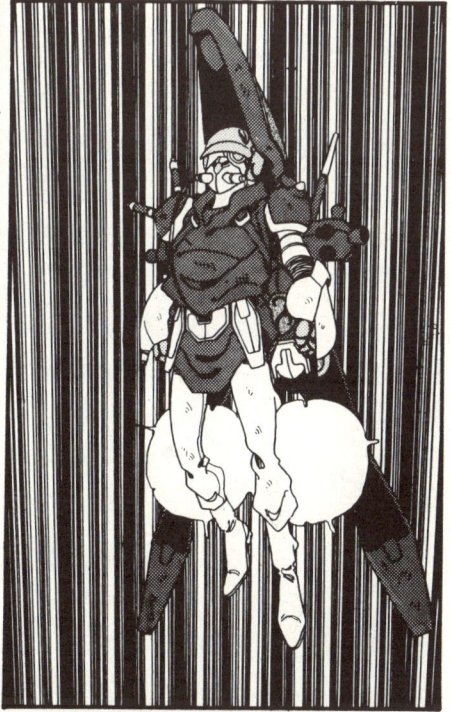

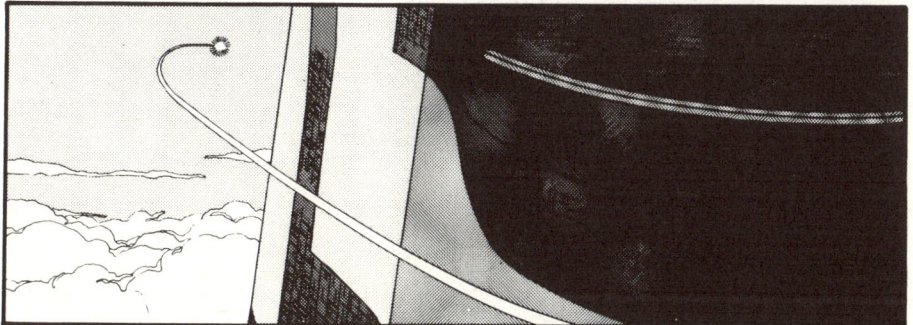

GREAT...

YOOSH

WAH!

5370

HI.

BYOW

212

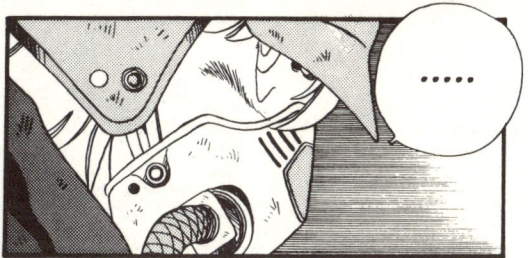

WHA--?!

BOM!

DAMN YOU!

PYEW

ZHAP

GREY!!

CAN YOU HEAR ME?

IF YOU CAN HEAR ME-- HURRY!

I CAN'T HOLD THEM MUCH LONGER!

I'LL *BE* THERE! SAVE YOUR *OWN* PRETTY ASS!

WHY, GREY! YOU MAKE ME *BLUSH!*

HARD TO PICTURE A MACHINE BLUSHING.

I STILL HAVE A WOMAN'S BODY.

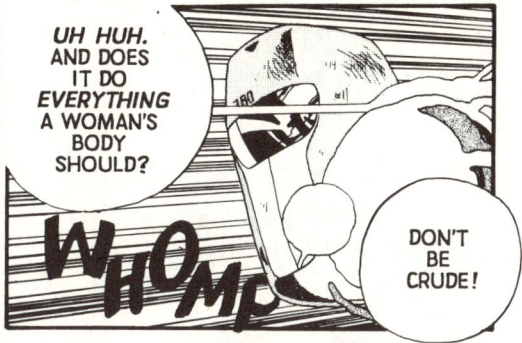

UH HUH. AND DOES IT DO *EVERYTHING* A WOMAN'S BODY SHOULD?

WHOMP

DON'T BE CRUDE!

REMIND ME TO STOP TRYING TO JOKE WITH MACHINES.

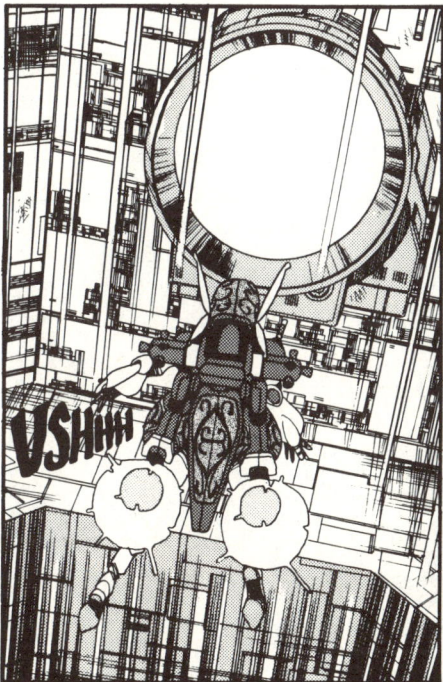

VSHiiiii

TIK TIK

TOO SLOW!

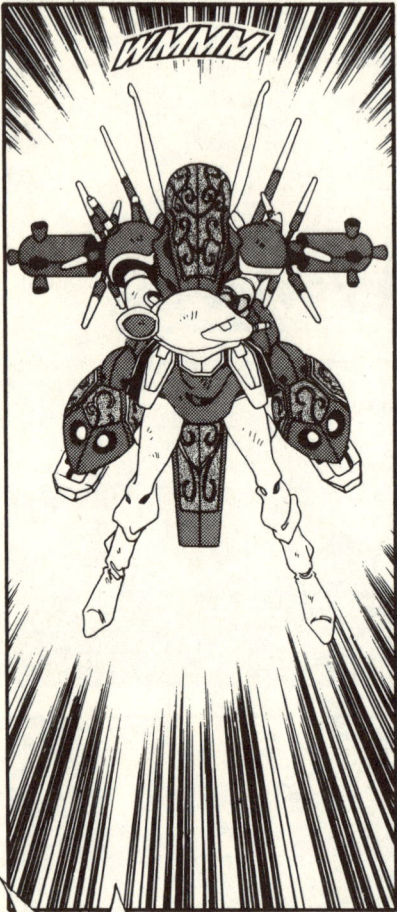

216

BM
BM
BM
BM
BM

FLY RIGHT OVER THE GUNSHIP!

THE DEAD SPOT IS DIRECTLY ABOVE IT.

ALL RIGHT...

OKAY, THAT'S GOOD, GOOD...

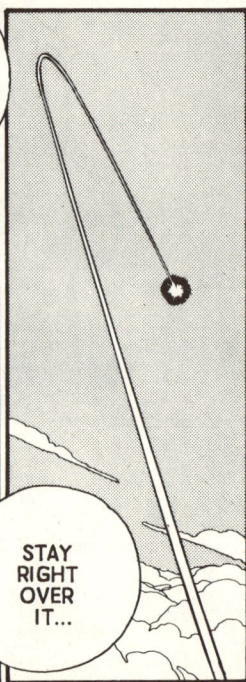

STAY RIGHT OVER IT...

IT'S THE SAME DAMN PATTERN!

DON'T UNDER-ESTIMATE THEM, GREY!

I SEE WHAT YOU MEAN...

TOY ISN'T SO EASY TO DEAL WITH!

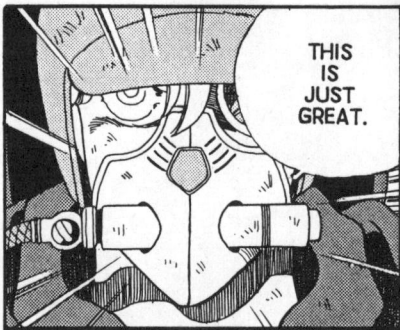

THIS
IS
JUST
GREAT.

DODO
DO
DO

BA
BA

OH
SHIT!

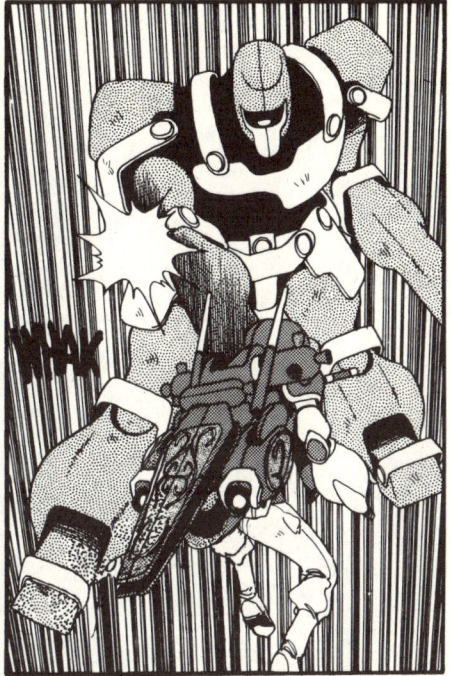

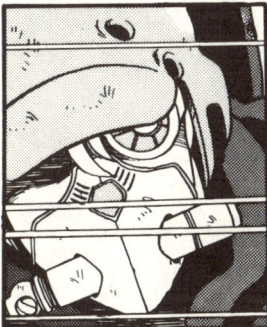

BASTARD...

HOLY--

ROKK!

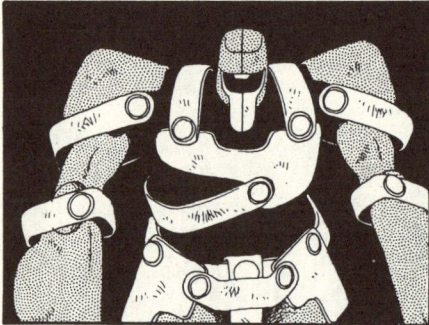

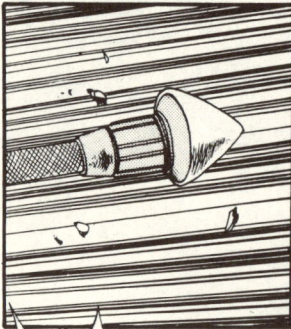

SNIKT

CHANK

GOD DAMN *MACHINE!*

222

ZZAP ZAP ZAP

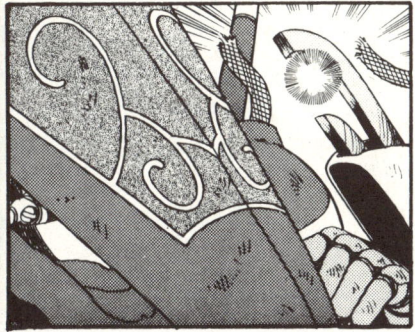

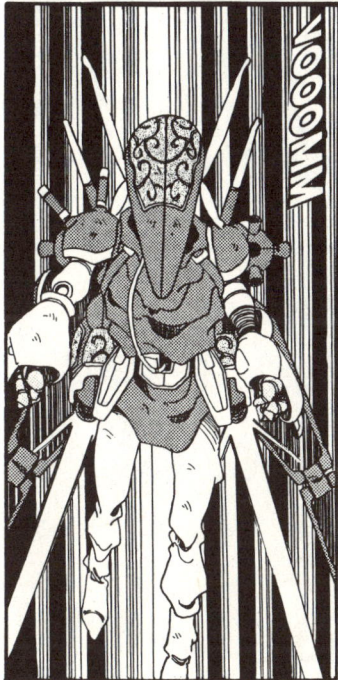

VOOOMM

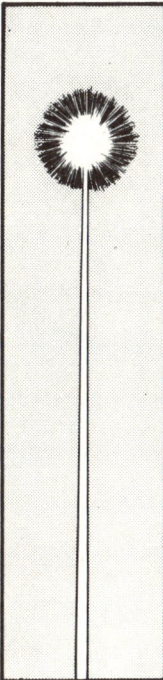

GREY!

SHAKE IT!

CLEAR OUT, LARÁ!

FOOSH

BM.

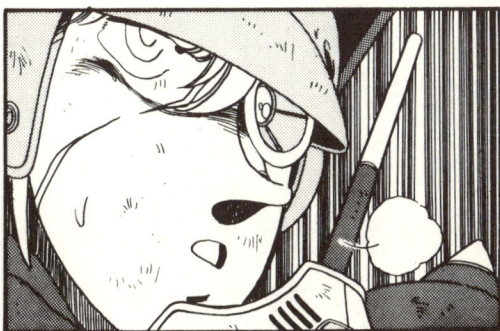

225

THAT WAS... REMARKABLE, GREY.

IT WAS THE FLIGHT-PACK THAT DID IT!

EXCEPT IT'S GOT A LITTLE TOO MUCH POWER TO CONTROL.

THAT PACK WORKS VERY WELL.

YOU ARE LIGHTER THAN SHIDARA.

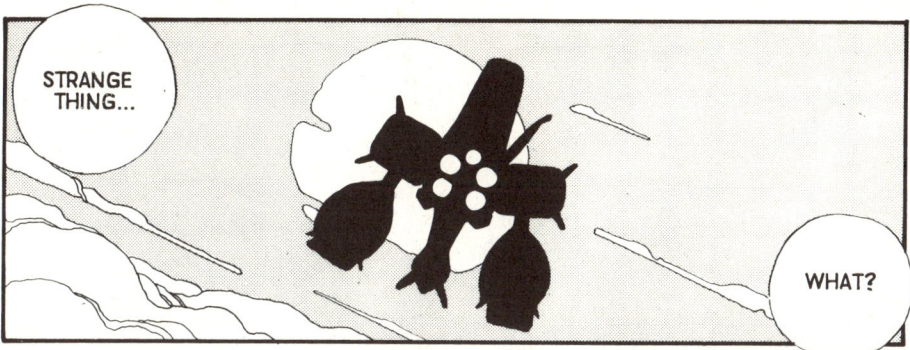

STRANGE THING...

WHAT?

THERE WERE NO MEN IN THERE.

ON THAT MONSTER SHIP... NOT ONE MAN.

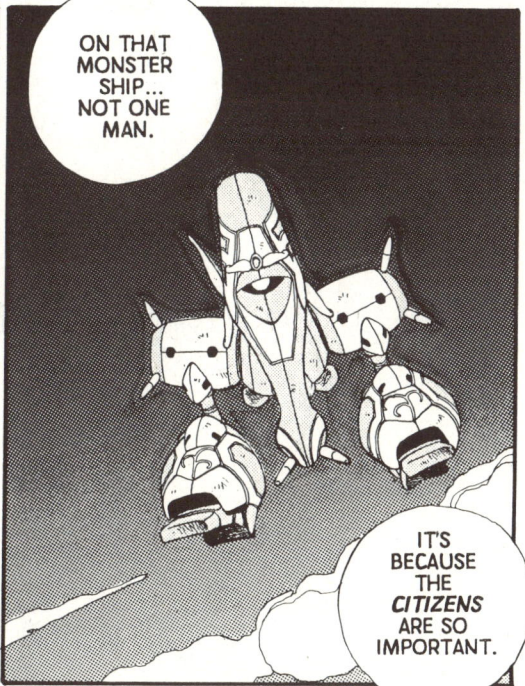

.....

IT'S BECAUSE THE *CITIZENS* ARE SO IMPORTANT.

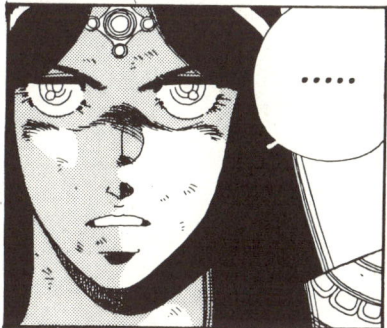

THE ONLY DUTY FOR ALL THOSE GREAT SOLDIERS WITH THEIR GREAT RECORDS IS GUARDING *TOY.*

IT'S PITIFUL, DON'T YOU THINK?

IF YOU CAN PROMISE MEN A VICTORY...

...THEN ISN'T IT TRUE...

...THAT MEN WILL *WANT* WAR?

SO ANYWAY...

EVEN GOING UP AGAINST THOSE CITIZENS, I...

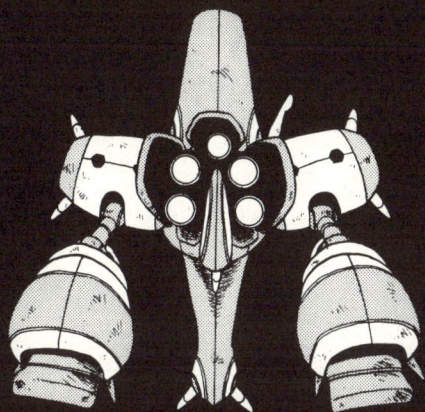

Approach Ten: The City, Part 2

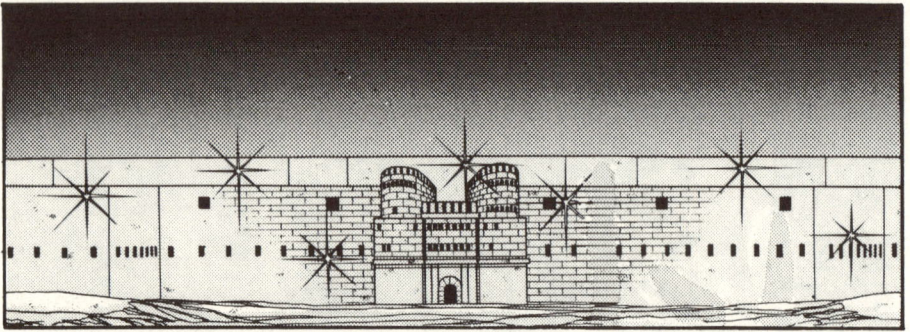

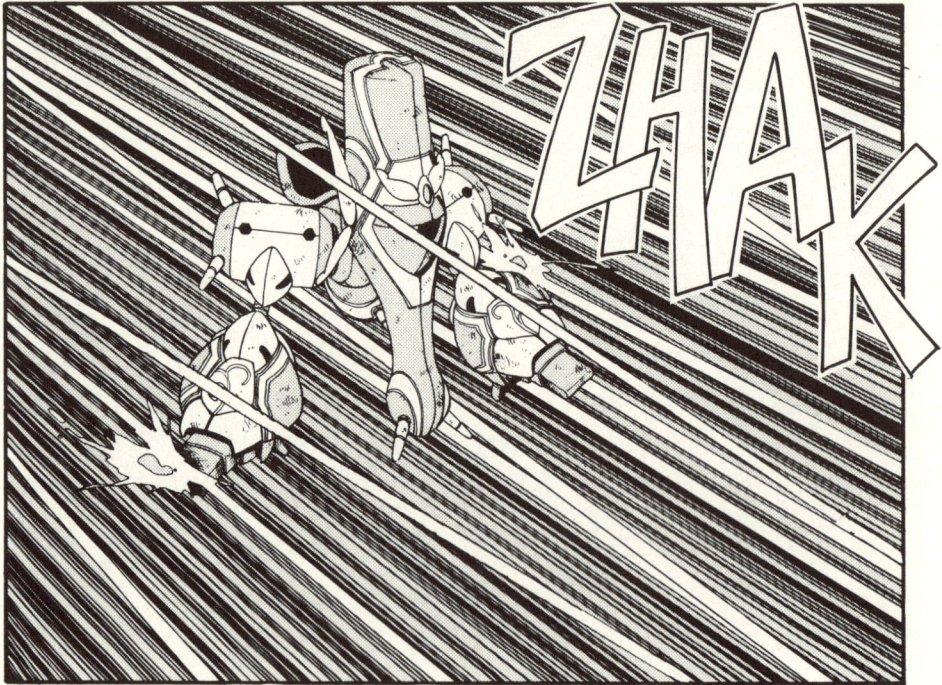

NO CHOICE ANYMORE, LARA. LET'S *GO!*

I'M WITH YOU.

THERE'S NO WAY...

I'VE GOT TO ATTACK FROM *OUTSIDE.*

.....

KEEP CHARGING STRAIGHT, LARA.

I'LL COVER YOU.

ROGER, GREY.

DON'T TRY TOO HARD. THE CITY HAS TWO OUTSIDE WALLS. IF YOU DON'T THINK YOU CAN BREACH 'EM BOTH-- *GIVE UP.*

IN THAT CASE... I'LL JUST CRASH INTO THE WALLS.

GONNA COMMIT SUICIDE?

I HAVE MY OWN FLIGHT-PACK, GREY.

WELL, ISN'T THAT A COMFORT?

READY TO *EJECT!*

WHOA! EJECTED TOO *SOON!*

VWOOSH

NEVER HAD A PROBLEM WITH *THAT* BEFORE.

ASK ANY OF MY GIRL-FRIENDS.

I'M SURE I DON'T CARE.

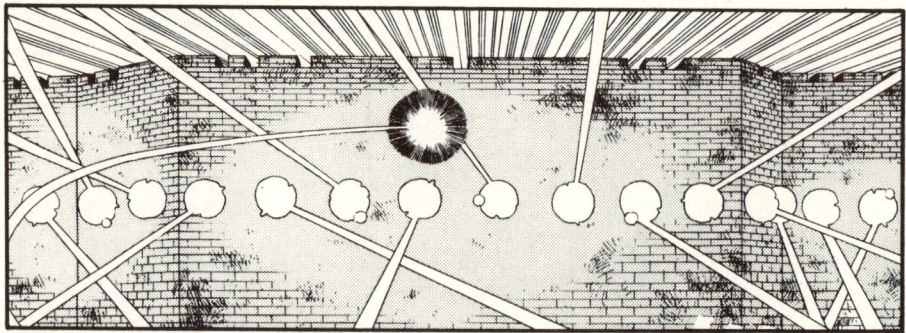

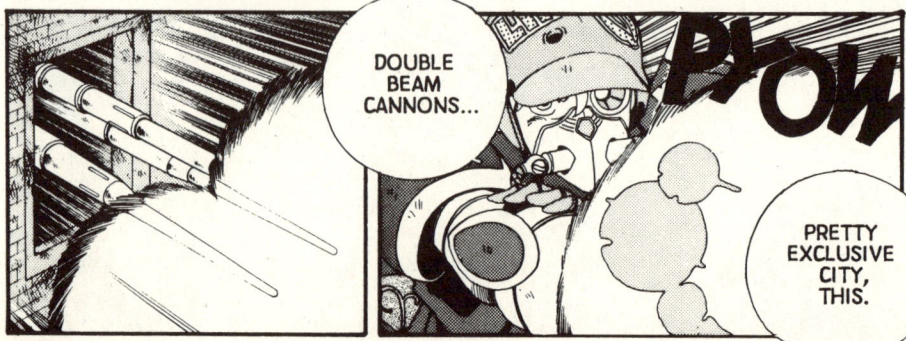

238

THEY'RE DEFENSELESS AGAINST ATTACK FROM THE *SIDE.*

BUH-WOOM

AND *THAT* MEANS...

UH *HUH.* I GET IT...

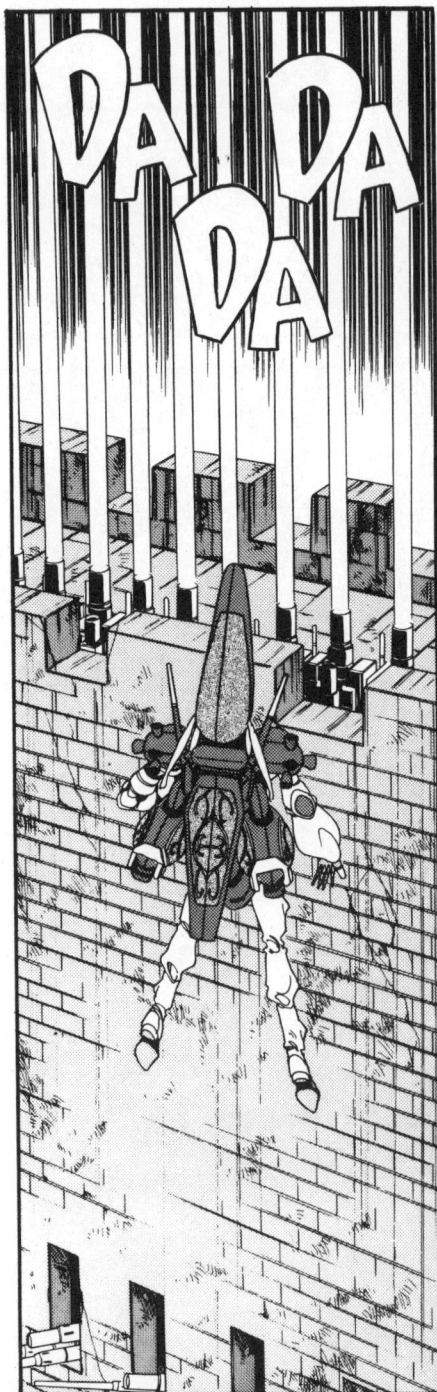

EJECT, LARA!

I INTEND TO!

KLAK

VWISH

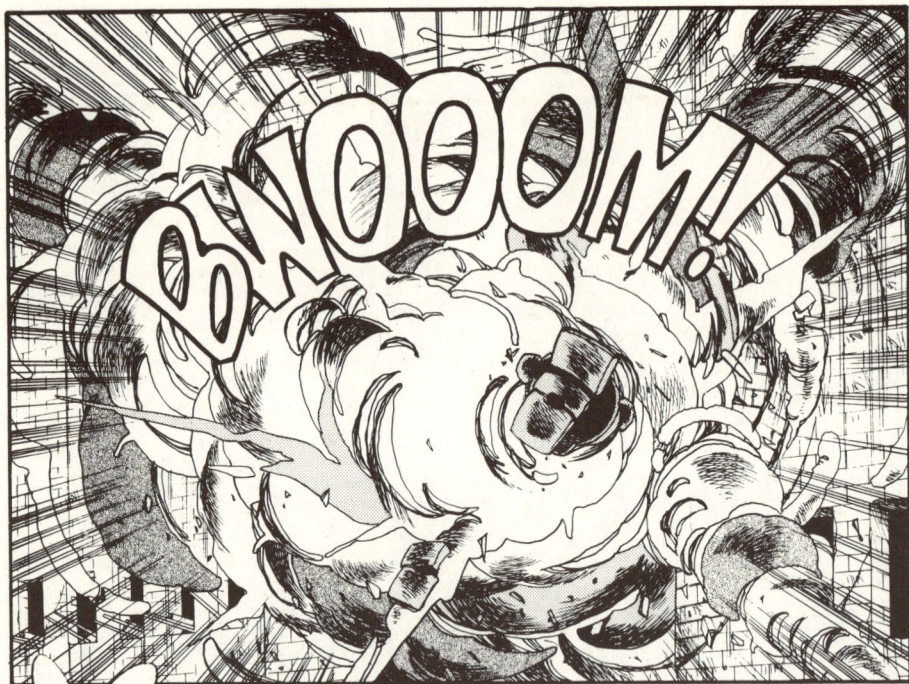

BWOOOM!

LET'S *ATTACK*, GREY!

FINE-- BUT THROUGH THE *GATE!*

THINK. TOY WILL BE EXPECTING A STRIKE FROM OVER THE WALLS.

YES... OF COURSE.

243

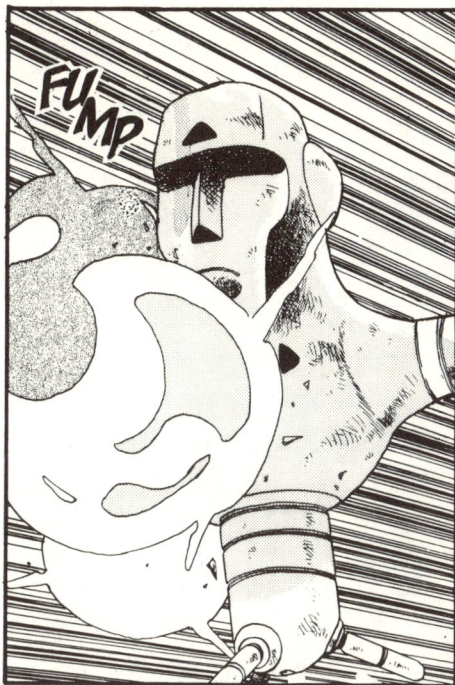

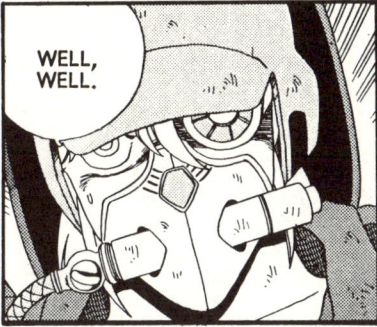

TOO
SLOW!

GREY!!

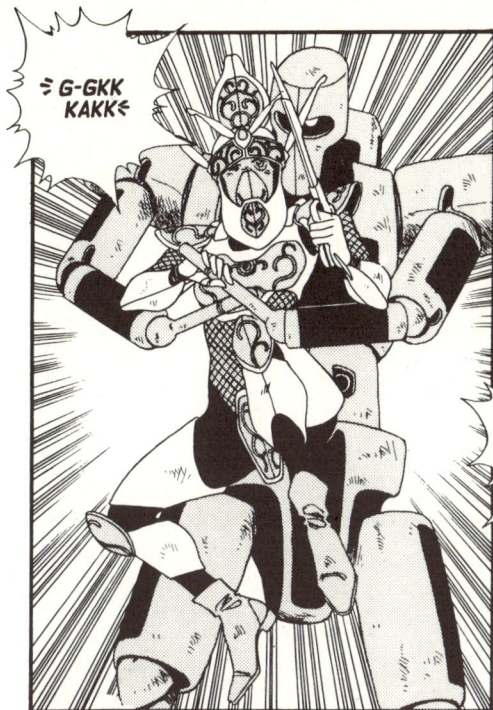

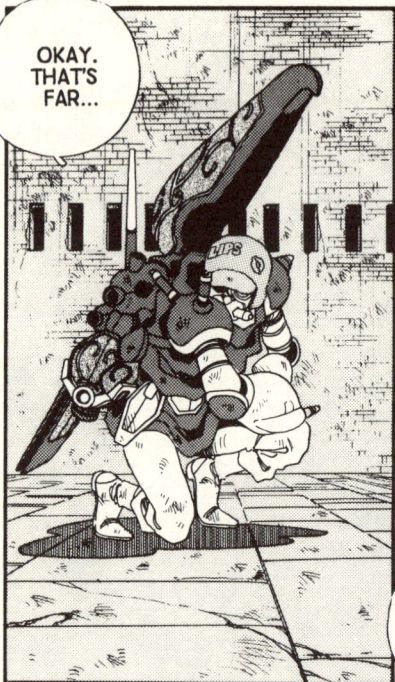

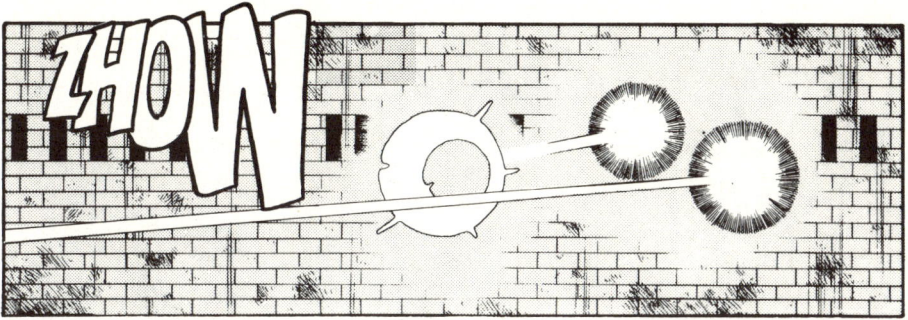

THERE'S THE *GATE,* GREY!

LET'S HIT IT TOGETHER.

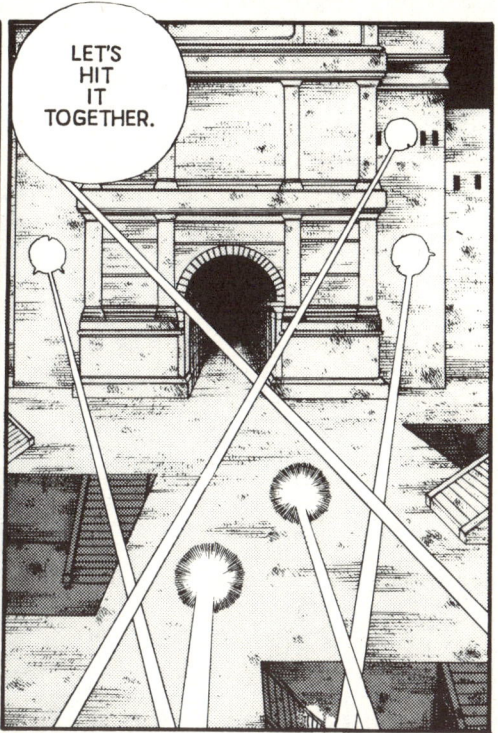

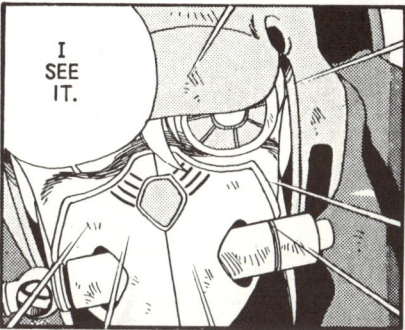

I SEE IT.

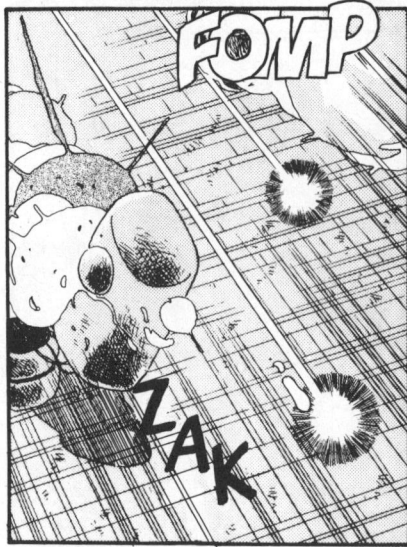

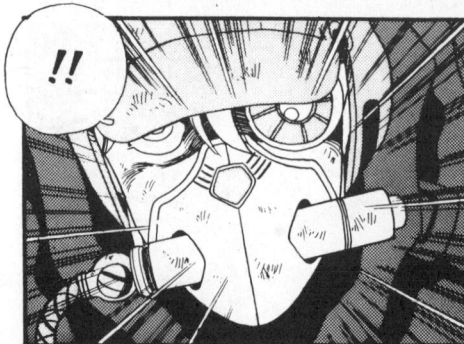

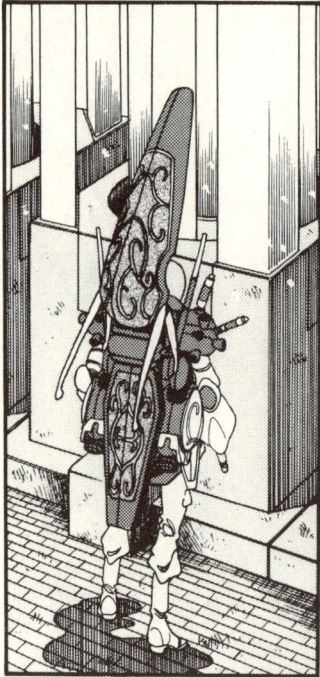

NOW WHAT? WIPE EVERY ONE OF THESE *BEAM-SHOOTERS*...

...AND DODGE 'EM AT THE SAME TIME?

IMPOSSIBLE, GREY...

KLAK

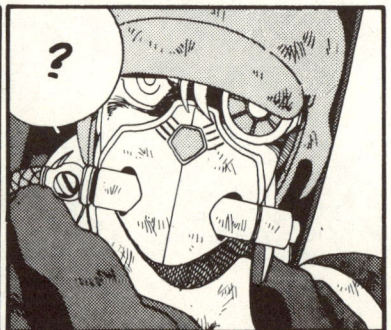

?

255

EEYAA--

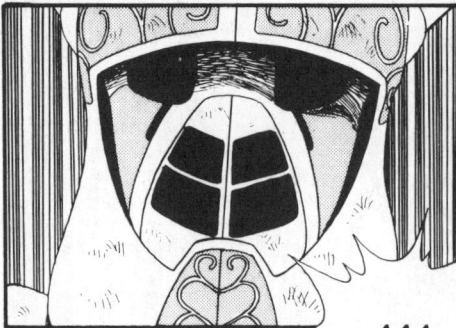

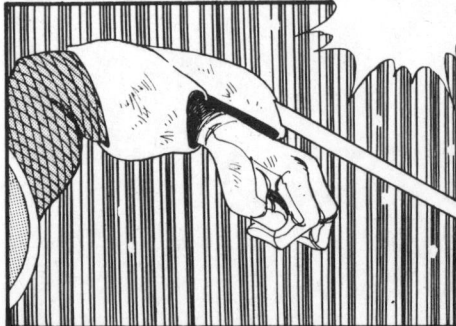

--AAA--

IT'S... IT'S OKAY NOW...

...GREY.

WELL, WELL. HOW INSPIRING.

I DID IT FOR *YOU*, GREY.

BYEW

YOU GOT A GLITCH IN YOUR COMPUTER BRAIN?

POOM

YOU DID IT TO DESTROY *TOY*.

WELL... PERHAPS *SO...*

LIKE IT SHOULD BE.

CAN YOU WALK?

I'M FINE... THANK YOU.

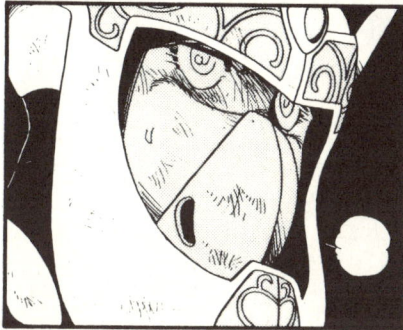

Approach Eleven: TOY

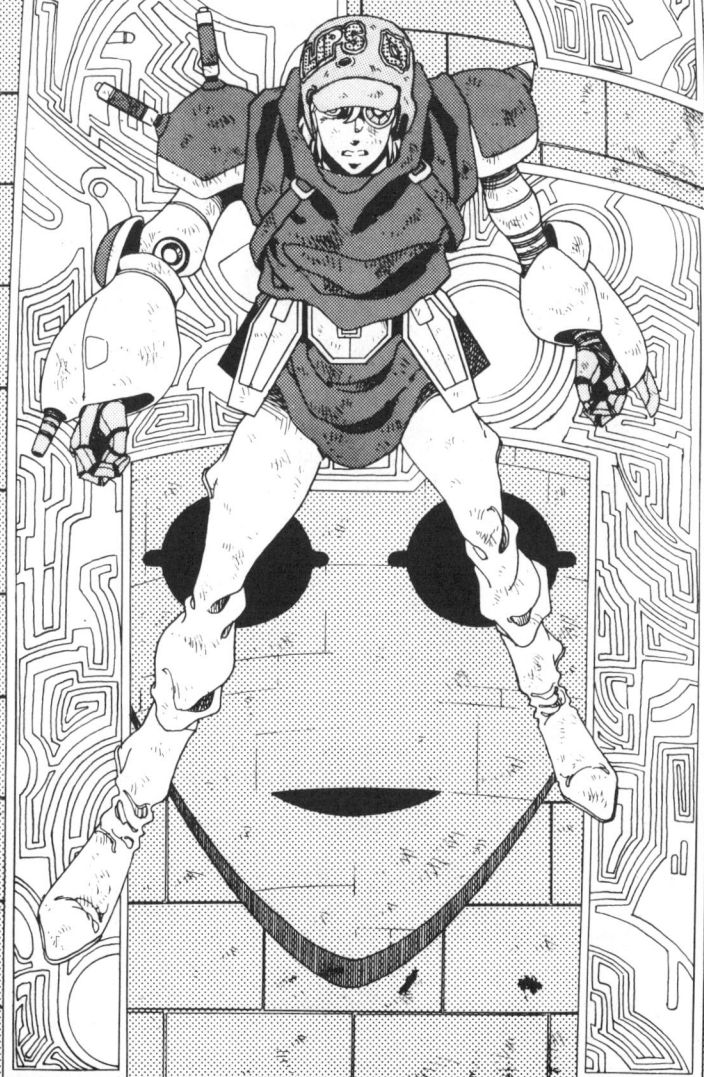

LARA!!

SHAK

SHAK

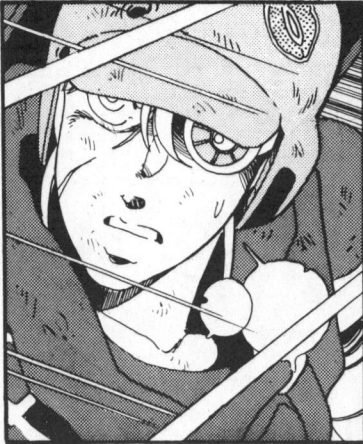

CHIK

QUEEE

BIP

BIBIP

DAMN.

HEY. YOU STILL ALIVE?

FOR... THE MOMENT.

YOUR CHEST?

BEAM MUST HAVE GRAZED... HEART MECHANISM.

HOW LONG CAN YOU LAST?

I...I CAN'T SAY, BUT...

...NOT LONG.

GREY!

CHAK

HERE. GRAB HOLD OF THIS.

266

THEY PROTECTING *TOY?*

EVERYBODY'S THE SAME. COVERING HIS *OWN* ASS, HIS OWN LIFE...

NO. THE *CITY*... AND THEIR LIVES...

...AS CITIZENS.

...PEOPLE IN THE TOWNS, IN THE CITY, DOESN'T MATTER.

AND I WAS THE SAME.

SO WHAT DO WE DO?

MY BODY... DOESN'T SEEM TO MOVE... ANYMORE.

WHAT?

I'M... SORRY, GREY.

OKAY. SO LET'S EXCHANGE FLIGHT-PACKS.

THIS FLIGHT-PACK HAS *LEGS*.

I WANT YOU FIGHTING 'TIL YOU DIE...OR 'TIL WE FINALLY ICE *TOY*.

I WILL HELP YOU GREY...BUT... DON'T DO THIS FOR *ME*...

HA! IF SHIDARA COULD HEAR YOU NOW!

LET'S GO.

SHIT!!

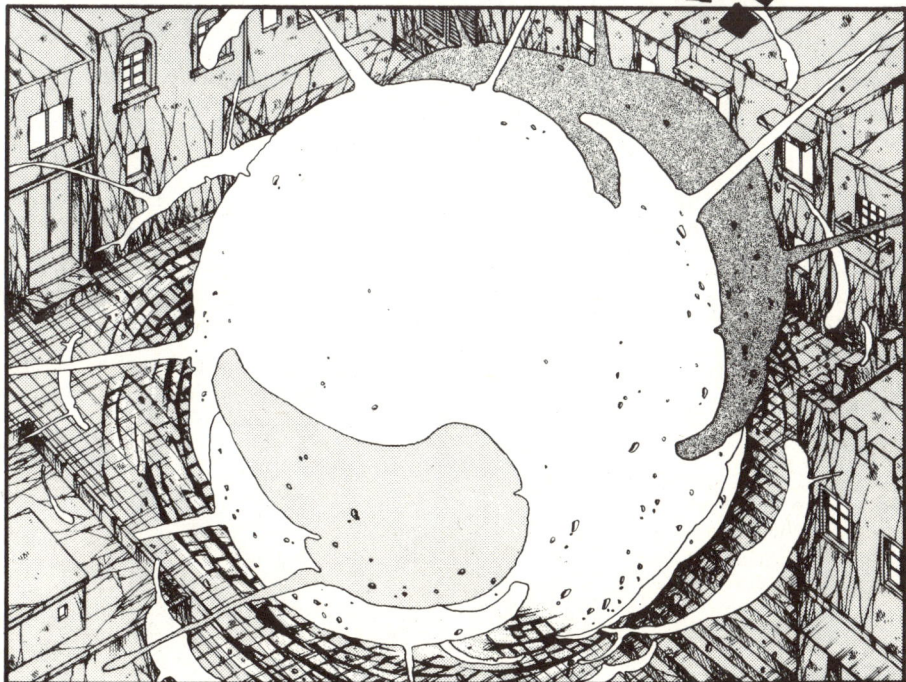

GR-GREY?

WHAT THE HELL HAPPENED?

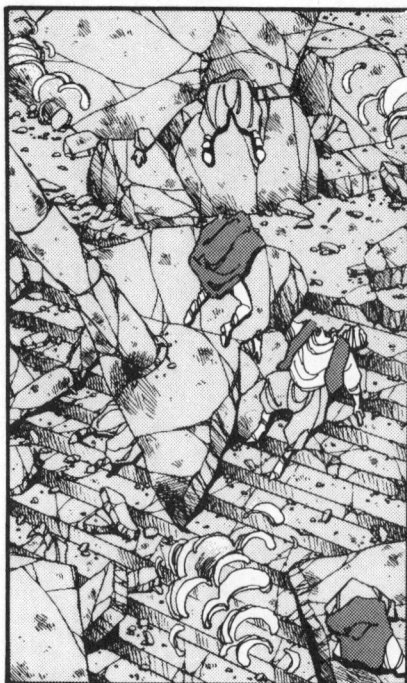

WHAT... WHAT...

THEY'RE *DOLLS?*

THIS ONE...

...AND THAT ONE, TOO...

...AND THIS...

ALL OF THEM. ALL DOLLS?

WHAT THE HELL'S GOING ON?

YOU MEAN CITIZENS... ARE DOLLS?!

PAK

CHAK

LOOK OUT!

CITIZENS ARE...

PYEN

...ARE ALL...

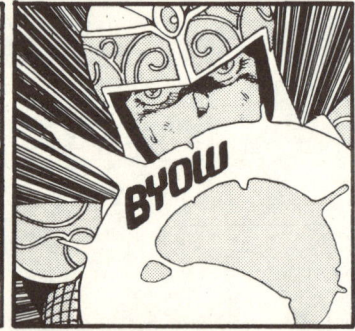

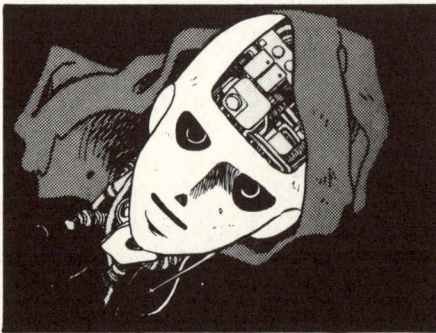

ARE WE GONNA LEARN THE TRUTH...

...IF WE GET THERE?

IF WE MEET *TOY?*

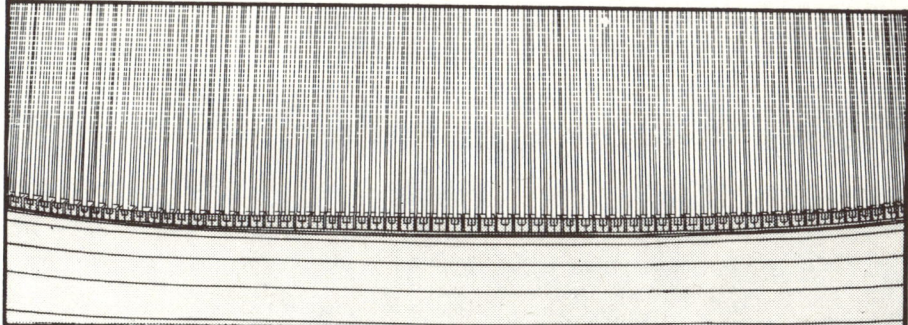

...DEAR GREY.

GOOD... GOOD-BYE...

.....

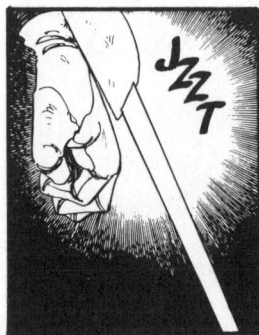
JZZT

JZZT

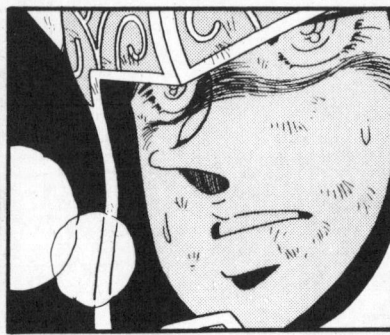

KRAK!

RMRMRMRMRM

SABMBOOM

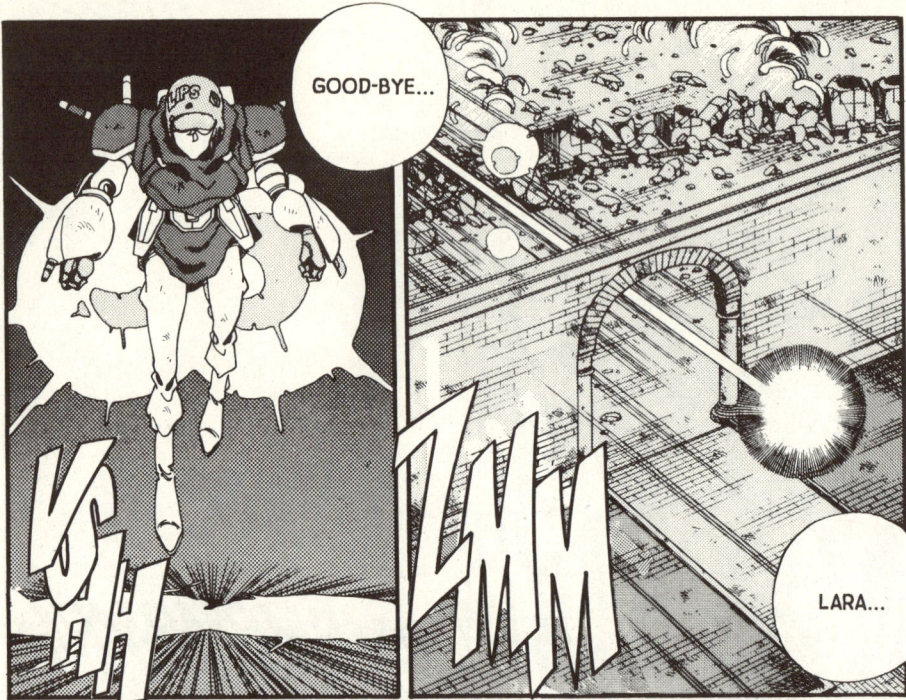

BEHIND THAT *WALL* --

HYAHH!

PYEW

WHOOM

JZZZ

ZZOK!

CHK

TFA 404953B. "GREY."

ASSIGNATION: TOWN 303, PEC-300 BATTALION, SQUAD 16422. CONFIRMED.

VOOOSH

PLEASE COME IN.

THANK YOU FOR COMING, GREY.

IT'S BEEN A HARD TRIP FOR YOU, HASN'T IT?

I'M PLEASED TO MEET YOU TOO, GREY.

THERE ARE THINGS I WOULD LIKE TO ASK YOU.

YOU, AND SHIDARA, AND LARA.

NOTHING'S HARD IF IT MEANS MEETING YOU... *TOY.*

THAT'S GOOD, 'CAUSE THERE'S *ONE* THING I WANT TO ASK YOU.

OH? AND WHAT IS THAT, GREY?

ALL THE CITIZENS-- THE *CLASS A TROOPERS*-- WHERE ARE THEY?

WHY ARE ALL THE CITIZENS *DOLLS?*

NOW, GREY. WE KNOW THAT MANKIND WANTS TO BECOME EXTINCT. DO CREATURES WHO WISH TO DIE REALLY NEED A PARADISE?

YOU MEAN... THERE'VE *NEVER* BEEN ANY CLASS A TROOPERS... FROM THE *START?*

OH, HOW PERCEPTIVE YOU ARE.

TOY, YOU CAN'T REALLY *BELIEVE--*

284

--YOU CAN'T BELIEVE THAT MANKIND "WANTS TO BECOME EXTINCT"!

BUT MOST PEOPLE SIMPLY WON'T ACKNOWLEDGE THAT.

IT'S SELF-DELUSION, THAT'S ALL.

THE CITY'S VALUE IS TO LET THEM SEE THAT.

IF WE DO-- WHAT'S THE POINT OF THIS *CITY?*

NO, GREY.

WON'T ACKNOWLEDGE...

MAYBE IT'S *TRUE* SOMEHOW...

...BUT IF IT IS, WHY *SHOULD* WE ACKNOWLEDGE IT?

MANKIND WANTS TO BECOME EXTINCT.

PEOPLE ARE *HAPPY,* NOT SEEING THAT!

BUT GREY. I ACKNOWLEDGED IT.

I AM DOING THIS FOR MANKIND.

SIMPLY TO FULFILL YOUR DESIRE.

STOP THIS LUNACY...

STOP THIS LUNACY!

KRAK!

!!

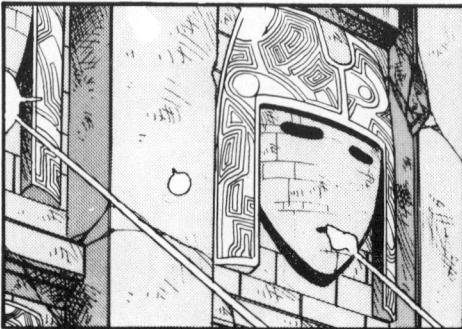

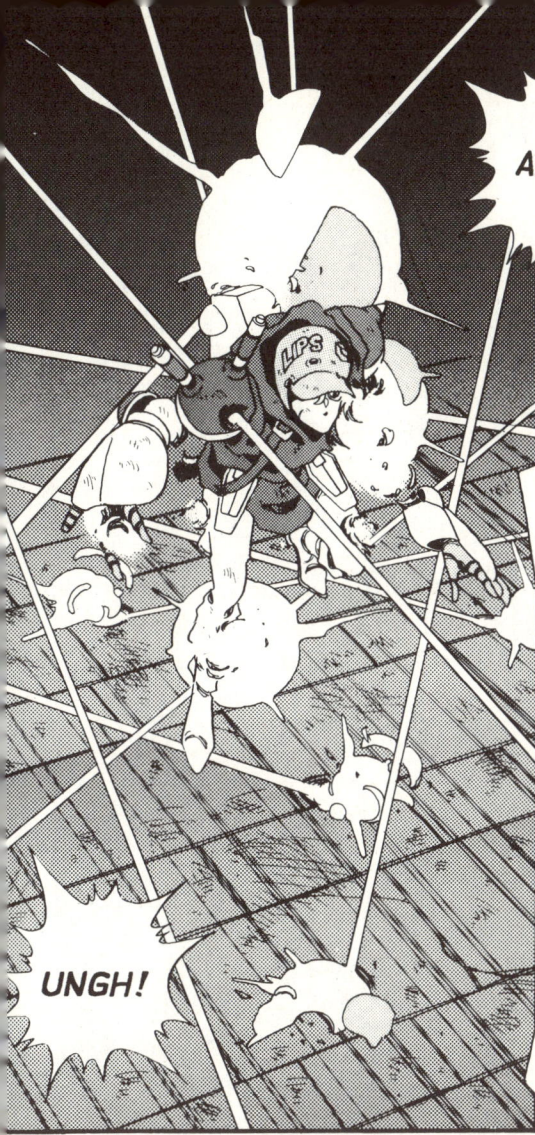

AAAA!

IT'S USELESS, GREY.

I'M PERFECT, YOU SEE.

ZHUN

I'M THE TRUTH.

I'M THE ABSOLUTE.

UNGH!

I'M GOD, GREY.

...GOD...

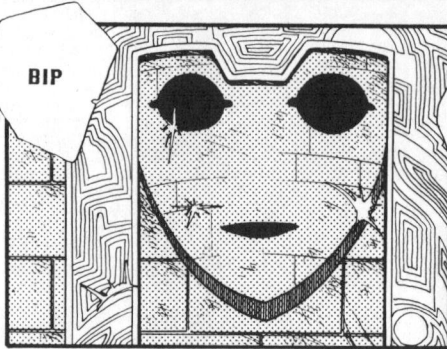

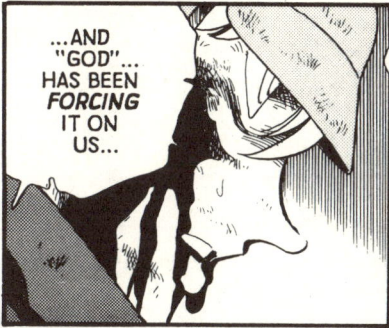

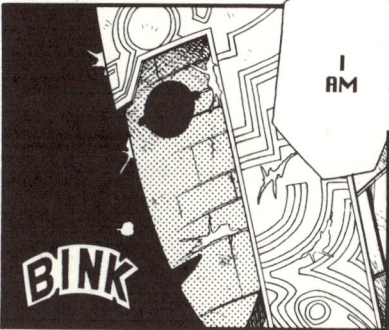

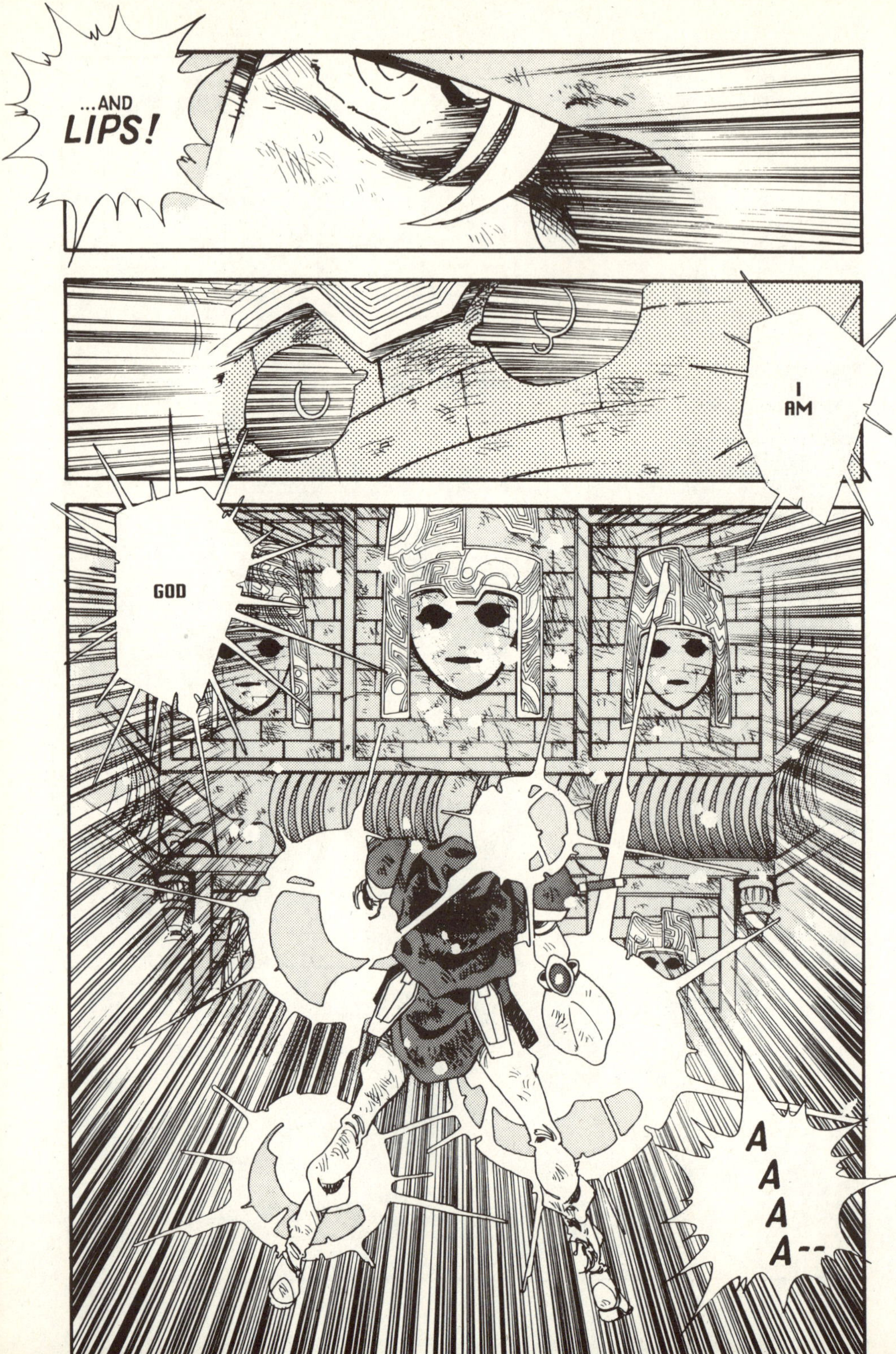
...AND LIPS!
I AM
GOD
AAAA--

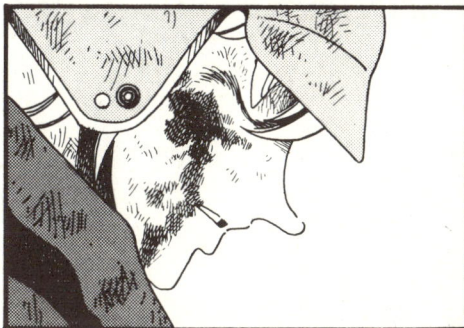
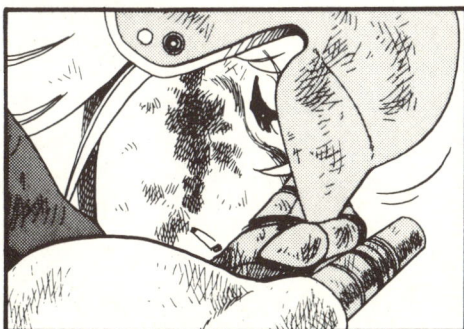

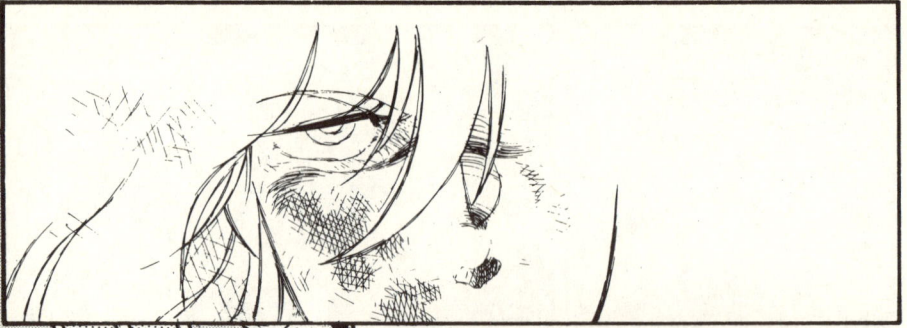

THE END

A Look Back at Grey

Gerard Jones

Despite all the elaborate battles, titanic machines, screaming sound effects, baroque terminology, and intricate penwork, *Grey* is ultimately a very sparse, almost minimalist, manga series.

Its cast of characters is not large; when all the machines are subtracted, its cast of human characters is quite small indeed. All of them but one flash in and out of the storyline leaving scarcely any impression. They help a little to move the protagonist on his way, although we suspect that he would have moved that way anyway. They die, and he pauses a moment to mourn some of them, but we never get the sense that their deaths matter very much to what happens next. They are only additional entries in a vast catalogue of amoral and emotionless offenses committed by machines against men.

Ultimately, it is simply the story of Grey Death marching across the desert to confront the ruler of the world, all alone.

I spent nine months involved with these characters, as the "rewriter" of *Grey*. My job was to take a literal English translation and brush it up colloquially, which included giving

the characters their distinctive speaking styles. I found very little in the characters, as people, to keep me interested in them. At first I took this to be a weakness of the series, but on looking back over it as a whole, I realized that it would probably have been weaker, in fact, if I had been able to find them interesting.

There are four human characters truly essential to the plot: Grey Death himself, who ultimately solves the riddle of his machine-driven future earth and strives to destroy its electronic despot; Lips, the one love of Grey's life, whose death gives him the peculiar fatalism and cynicism that makes him what he is; Red, Grey's one friend, whose abduction derails Grey from the normal course of a Trooper and sends him off into those desolate regions where truth is found; and Robert J. Dimitri, a computer scientist who played a crucial role in creating this hideous world and who gives Grey the information he needs to master it. (There are others along the way, but they are little more than obstacles to Grey's quest, or demonstrations of the story's principles. Even Nova, who appears in *Grey's* pages more than

anyone except the hero himself, is ultimately just someone for Grey Death to talk to as he pieces together a picture of his world.)

Their functions are clear and essential: Lips is the one who jars Grey out of his despairing complacency as one of the earth's countless disposable, pointless "People"; Red is the one who jars him from the path which "Big Mama" has laid down for the discontented, a path that proves to be just as much of a dead-end as the narrow cycle followed by the common folk; and Robert is that constant figure of all heroes' journeys, the odd, even supernatural, helper who pops up when help seems least likely, who provides the final tools that enable the hero to triumph, but who is unable to enjoy the triumph himself. And Grey Death, of course, *is* the story. He is the hero, the would-be liberator of the world, the revealer of truth.

What's interesting about these four figures is that all of them essentially do their work through death. Lips is killed before the series even begins. Red disappears, apparently dead, very early, to give the plot its one decisive turning-point. Robert is obsolete, an anachronism, clinging to time not his own; his aid to Grey will result in killing his own legacy, his own "other self," his own purpose in the world. And Grey, seemingly, is marching toward a suicidal confrontation; not "it's either you or me, Big Mama," but instead, "it's got to be you *and* me."

Nothing has been left to these people but death, and that's how it has to be in Yoshihisa Tagami's dismal future. The world has been made a desert, not by accident but by design. Mankind has been manipulated into endless, aimless warfare, and every human institution has been reconstructed toward the furtherance of slaughter. Death is the aim of the machines who rule mankind; death is the one defining experience of human life. It is metaphorically perfect that death should be the only device through which the world might be changed.

That's why the characters in *Grey* should not be very interesting. That's why they should not be complex and changeable, vital and growing. They are walking corpses, moving through a world of windowless corridors and animate machines that lead them toward the same destination, the final dehumanization. If they show any occasional sparks of life, it is only because a momentary confluence of circumstances has made it possible for them to give their deaths a little meaning, to transform their corpses into soil for a more vivid world still far in the future.

It may not have been Tagami's intention to make these characters less than fully human. But by the same token it can't be completely accidental that he lavished so much more imagination and attention on his machines than on his humans. In his world, the humans are adjuncts of the machines. Grey Death, with his externally determined, inexorable march toward a showdown with his master, is not so much a man exercising free will as he is a malfunction. The story of *Grey* is not one of man triumphing over his creations, but of a systemic collapse in which the machines destroy themselves with their own flawed, rigid logic.

The message of *Grey* is not that mankind can control its machines, but that we can simply outlive them.